Gorian and his men were here for the Teeth of the Ice Bear. And, since they had the assistance of some sorcerer—who presumably told the Stygian responsible for its theft about the crown in the first place—they would have some idea where to find it.

Not much to go on, Kral thought. But better than nothing, which was what they had had only moments before.

"So we stay with them?" Mikelo asked, just as Donial was about to.

"Yes," Kral replied. "And when they find the crown, we take it instead."

"There are more of them, and better armed," Donial said. "And they have magic on their side."

Kral chuckled, without humor. "Did I say it would be easy?"

D1601719

Millions of readers have enjoyed Robert E. Howard's stories about Conan. Twelve thousand years ago, after the sinking of Atlantis, there was an age undreamed of when shining kingdoms lay spread across the world. This was an age of magic, wars, and adventure, but above all this was an age of heroes! The Age of Conan series features the tales of other legendary heroes in Hyboria.

AGE OF CONAN
HYBORIAN ADVENTURES

MARAUDERS
Volume III

DAWN OF THE ICE BEAR

Jeff Mariotte

ACE BOOKS, NEW YORK

THE BERKLEY PUBLISHING GROUP
Published by the Penguin Group
Penguin Group (USA) Inc.
375 Hudson Street, New York, New York 10014, USA
Penguin Group (Canada), 90 Eglinton Avenue East, Suite 700, Toronto, Ontario M4P 2Y3, Canada
(a division of Pearson Penguin Canada Inc.)
Penguin Books Ltd., 80 Strand, London WC2R 0RL, England
Penguin Group Ireland, 25 St. Stephen's Green, Dublin 2, Ireland (a division of Penguin Books Ltd.)
Penguin Group (Australia), 250 Camberwell Road, Camberwell, Victoria 3124, Australia
(a division of Pearson Australia Group Pty. Ltd.)
Penguin Books India Pvt. Ltd., 11 Community Centre, Panchsheel Park, New Delhi—110 017, India
Penguin Group (NZ), Cnr. Airborne and Rosedale Roads, Albany, Auckland 1310, New Zealand
(a division of Pearson New Zealand Ltd.)
Penguin Books (South Africa) (Pty.) Ltd., 24 Sturdee Avenue, Rosebank, Johannesburg 2196, South
Africa

Penguin Books Ltd., Registered Offices: 80 Strand, London WC2R 0RL, England

This is a work of fiction. Names, characters, places, and incidents either are the product of the author's imagination or are used fictitiously, and any resemblance to actual persons, living or dead,
business establishments, events, or locales is entirely coincidental. The publisher does not have any
control over and does not assume any responsibility for author or third-party websites or their
content.

DAWN OF THE ICE BEAR

An Ace Book / published by arrangement with Conan Properties International, LLC.

PRINTING HISTORY
Ace edition / June 2006

Copyright © 2006 by Conan Properties International, LLC.
Cover art by Justin Sweet.
Interior text design by Stacy Irwin.

ISBN: 0-441-01392-9

ACE
Ace Books are published by The Berkley Publishing Group,
a division of Penguin Group (USA) Inc.,
375 Hudson Street, New York, New York 10014.
ACE and the "A" design are trademarks belonging to Penguin Group (USA) Inc.

PRINTED IN THE UNITED STATES OF AMERICA

10 9 8 7 6 5 4 3 2 1

*Dedicated to my son David, who has yet to discover
the wonder of sword & sorcery . . .
but who will.*

PACHENIA

VILAYET SEA

ISLE OF IRON STATUES

HYRKANIA

KHITAI

NAHUI

ZUBAI

KOSALA

VENDHYA

MISTY ISLES

S OF PEARL

S O U T H E R N   S E A

Acknowledgments

Thanks to Theodore Bergquist, Fredrik Malmberg, Jeff Conner, and Matt Forbeck, for faith and inspiration. To Ginjer Buchanan, for follow-through. And to my family, to my friends, and to the Peraltas, the Swisshelms, and the Chiricahuas, for being outside and keeping me sane and centered through it all.

1

A SCORCHING SUN seared the windswept Stygian landscape. The temperature climbed to unseasonable heights, even for this normally torrid land. Flowers wilted on their vines. Small pools of water evaporated overnight, leaving chalky mineral rings where they'd been.

Shehkmi al Nasir was barely aware of the dramatic change in the weather. He had not ventured beyond the walls of his own compound in weeks. The magics he had been working were wearing on him, so now he sought relaxation. Lounging in a deep copper tub, the sorcerer allowed three slave girls to bathe him, in water scented with oils and spices. Two of the girls were Kushites, the third the youngest niece of a Hyrkanian prince. She was a girl of surpassing beauty, with flame-red hair and flashing emerald eyes. Like the others—also beauties, but without her royal blood—she was dressed in only the scantiest silk breeches, lest her garb get soaked by the bathwater.

If any of the girls found him repulsive, with his tattooed, scarred face, his slashed-away earlobes, his vulturelike head, they knew better than to show it. Al Nasir was not known for his mercy or understanding. Everyone in his household had heard stories of his fearsome flights of rage, and they tried hard not to incite them.

Just now, his attention was not on the girls, lovely as they were. His thoughts were far away, on the ship that wended toward him carrying a rare prize. He had researched the strange Pictish crown that the Aquilonian mage Kanilla Rey had asked him about. He'd had to scour the most ancient texts he had: scrolls that he feared would turn to dust in his hands, old brittle-paged volumes. Finally, in a book with no title at all, but just an unknown symbol burned into its binding of human skin, he found that which he sought. The crown had a special significance to the Picts, but it had been around since long before the Great Cataclysm. Lemurians had known of it, and their songs spoke of its power. Atlanteans had coveted it. Battles had been fought for possession of the crown, and thousands had died in quest of it. How it finally came into possession of the Picts was not recorded, nor was it known where they kept it.

What he could surmise was that it was an object of great power—too great to be left to the savage Picts. They claimed it, but it was no more theirs than the sun or the moon was.

And soon it would belong to Shehkmi al Nasir. He was already a tremendously potent sorcerer. Whether this would give him the ability to challenge Thoth Amon's status as the greatest of Stygian mages, he knew not.

Even if it didn't, it would firmly ensconce him in second place. In a land dedicated to the pursuit of the dark arts, that was still a position to be valued. He would be respected, feared throughout the land, as he had never been before.

Shehkmi al Nasir chuckled dryly. The sound of his awful laughter raised goose bumps on the flesh of the girls who washed him.

EVERYONE CALLED THE ship the *Restless Heart,* even though the name *Barachan Spur* had been painted on her. But the *Spur* had been the name the Argossean pirates who had tried to commandeer her had called her by. Since they were all dead, or back on the coast of Shem, the surviving sailors of the original *Restless Heart,* and those of her passengers who yet lived, used the ship's original name. Most of their number, including the ship's Captain Ferrin, were buried back in Shem. Gorian of Aquilonia was in command now. He had magic at his disposal, which he had used to dispatch the buccaneers. His small troop of mercenaries already swore fealty to him. Upon seeing his magic at work, the *Heart*'s original crew did the same.

The only ones on board who had not specifically

promised their allegiance to Gorian were Alanya and
Donial, the children of Invictus; their traveling companion Kral, a young Pict; and Mikelo, a Zingaran boy who
had been a captive of the pirates. Alanya, Donial, and
Kral were paying passengers. Mikelo, having been res-
cued from the Argosseans, had agreed to stay with the
others until they returned to Aquilonia, from which he
would make his own way home. But that would have to
wait. The *Restless Heart* was bound for Stygia, in the
opposite direction. Alanya hoped they all survived to
travel back the other way.

The four of them had been allowed to keep the cabin
that she, Donial, and Kral had rented at the journey's
beginning. There were four bunks in the cabin, so while
it was a squeeze, it was still more comfortable than the
crew's quarters. With the porthole open, fresh salt air
blew into the cabin, erasing the scents of four people
closely confined.

Alanya sat in her bunk now, staring off toward the
porthole and the cloudless blue sky beyond it, trying to
make sense of her stew of emotions. While she was
pleased that they were once again headed for Stygia,
where Kral hoped to find the Teeth of the Ice Bear, a
mystical crown stolen from his people by her uncle
Lupinius, she dearly wished she were back home in
Aquilonia. She wished, too, that her father had not been
killed—probably by Lupinius. She wished her brother
had not been forced to kill a man in battle. Since that
day, he had been even moodier and more sullen than
usual, if possible. She admired Kral, but believed he

barely noticed her, except as a traveling companion and helpmate. At the same time, she found Mikelo's fascination with her unnerving. He was younger than she, and she had learned that she preferred men without the patina of civilization that he wore. Kral, with the dark hair and skin common to the Picts, savage and natural, was much more to her liking.

It all piled up inside her like leaves in a courtyard on an autumn day. She sighed involuntarily. Mikelo, who had stayed in their cabin even though Kral and Donial had both gone on deck, glanced over at her. "Is something wrong?" he asked solicitously.

"No," she said. Even as she spoke she knew it was just a reflexive answer, far from the truth. In her fifteen years, had anything ever been more wrong? "Maybe. I think I am simply weary, and confused."

"Confused about what?" he pressed.

She didn't know how to put her flurry of thoughts and feelings into words, or even if she should try. "I don't know. Everything. It is all . . . too much, that's all."

"Can I ask a question?"

"Of course," she said, not bothering to point out that he had been asking them all along.

"Why are you going to Stygia? What is it you seek there? I spent part of last winter there, when Kunios had an arrangement to dock in Khemi for a trading expedition, and that was enough for a lifetime."

Alanya knew that he had asked Donial the same question. Her younger brother had declined to answer. He believed, as did Alanya, that because it was Kral's quest, it should be up to him to decide to tell others or not. She had spoken to Kral about it, however, and he had indicated that he had no reason to keep it a secret from Mikelo. By helping them try to escape, the Zingaran boy had earned his way into their little group. Kral suggested that they might need another ally, particularly one who had been to Stygia and knew some of the language. Next time he asked, Kral said, she should feel free to tell him. She had hoped it would be Kral himself that Mikelo would ask, so she wouldn't have to.

But he had, so she took a deep breath and began the explanation. "A crown was stolen from Kral's clan," she said. "A precious antiquity with some sort of mystical significance to the Picts. We believe it has been taken by some Stygian priests, who are bringing it to Stygia. We mean to find it so Kral can take it back to his home."

Mikelo was not satisfied with the quick explanation. "How did it come to be stolen?"

Another sigh. She had hoped not to have to tell the whole story again. But the ship was quiet, as ships go. Winds filled the sails, men knew their tasks and did them, water splashed rhythmically against the hull. So she crossed her legs, making herself comfortable on her bunk. Mikelo did the same. Once they were settled, she started from the beginning. Her meeting with Kral in the woods outside the settlement of Koronaka. Their discovery by Donial, who reported what he had seen to Lupinius, their uncle. Lupinius's overreaction, and the subsequent raid on the Pictish village, which she was now convinced had some ulterior motive. Lupinius's probable murder of her father and his theft of the crown. She hesitated a little before telling him of Kral's murderous assault on Koronaka as the "Ghost of the Wall." But Kral had given her permission to tell everything, so she did. She described the trip back to Tarantia, after Lupinius had left Koronaka in the dead of night. How he had taken over her father's house and been slain in it as he tried to sell the crown to a thief. How she, Donial, and Kral had found him, barely clinging to life, and called for help. The unexpected visit from King Conan, which impressed him almost as much as it still did her. And then how Kral had been arrested for Lupinius's murder and how they had broken him out of jail. Mikelo sat silently, his brown eyes wide with wonder, during the entire story. When she got to the part where a freak storm grounded the *Restless Heart* on a reef off the coast of Shem—which was where they had met Mikelo—he whistled.

"You have had some amazing adventures," he said.

"More than enough adventure for me," Alanya said. "I never sought adventure. I would happily spend the rest of my life at home in Tarantia."

Mikelo's nod made his thick shock of light brown hair bob. He was a slight boy, but his energy and vigor made up for any frailty. "Still, since you are just now on the way to Stygia, it will be some time before you can do that."

"I know," she said sadly. "You asked if something was wrong. I guess that's it. I wish, more than anything, that I was not here, that none of this had ever happened.

Except for the meeting Kral part. That was good. The rest of it has been nothing but trouble."

She knew that Mikelo, like most Zingarans, considered the Picts natural enemies. But in the days since the pirates he had traveled with had attacked the marooned crew and passengers of the *Restless Heart,* he had come to know Kral. As seemed to happen so often, Alanya thought, becoming acquainted with an individual made it hard to cling to one's preconceived notions of an entire people. He had not yet taken Kral into his heart as fully as she and Donial had, but he seemed more trusting and genuinely concerned for the Pict's welfare.

"I am sorry," he said, "that it has been such an ordeal for you."

She felt the rocking of the boat, listened to the creak of wood and the snap of sailcloth. She understood that her answer had been the facile one, leaving out more than it revealed. Had it really been so bad? Yes, there had been many times when she had feared for her life and those of her friends. There had been danger and terror, loss and profound sorrow.

But hadn't there been other things, too? Good things? Discoveries about herself and her friends? They had all tapped previously unknown reservoirs of courage, had demonstrated their trust and faith in one another time after time. Just when things looked most bleak, they had come through for each other.

Her throat was dry from talking, and she didn't think she could explain all that to Mikelo anyway. Instead of answering, she just offered him a shrug of her shoulders.

"Let's go on deck," she suggested. "Maybe Donial and Kral are doing something interesting." She knew the chances of that were slim indeed. Day followed night followed day on the ship, with nothing changing at all. Wind and water. Water and wind. The men doing the things sailors did.

Mikelo agreed, so together they left their cabin and climbed the wooden ladder to the upper deck. At first glance everything looked the same as ever. It took her a minute to locate Kral and Donial, but finally she spotted them at the bow, leaning over the edge. A loose shirt flapped over Kral's muscular torso, nearly covering the wounds there. Donial, a year younger than Alanya, looked small compared to Kral, but with his black hair and dark eyes he almost resembled the Pict more than he did his fair-skinned, blond, blue-eyed sister. She and Mikelo joined them.

"What are you doing here?" Alanya asked.

Kral turned to her, windblown and bronzed darker than ever by his time on the ship. His chest was bare, and the wound left there by the pirate captain Kunios was scabbed over and red. "Out there," he said. "Look straight ahead."

She looked. Water.

"What?" she asked.

"Look harder," Donial urged. "You'll see it."

She looked again. Water. But at the edge of it, perhaps a darker strip. "What is . . . ?"

"Stygia," Kral answered. "That, lady, is Stygia."

One of the sailors overheard and rushed to the bow

himself. After a quick glance, he smiled, clapping Kral on the shoulder. Then he turned back toward the rest of the ship and cupped his hands to his mouth. "Land ho!" he shouted.

The call was picked up, echoed by others all across the vessel. "Land ho! Stygia off the bow!"

"At last," Kral said quietly. "Stygia, at last."

2

WITH STYGIA IN sight, things progressed at an agonizingly glacial pace. Having no official business in that land, they wanted to approach only when darkness would mask their arrival. Kral still had no idea what Gorian and his crew of mercenaries were after in Stygia. Nor did he particularly care, as long as their goals did not interfere with his. He knew he ran a risk—that if he and his friends abandoned the others as soon as they reached Stygia, they might have a difficult time getting home once he had the crown. But he was determined to ignore that problem for now. One thing at a time, and his first job was to get the crown in his hands. After that, he could worry about the next step.

So they tacked back and forth, wasting time, drawing slowly nearer the shore, until the sun set. Once it had, they doused all their lights and made straight for land. Now the hours passed slowly because they were so close, and even though they made progress, it was not fast enough for Kral's satisfaction. He was afraid morning would dawn before they were near enough.

But only a few hours had passed before he was called to the wheel to join Gorian and Allatin, the blond-bearded first mate. When he joined them, he could see that they were skirting the shore. City lights glowed in the near distance.

"There be Khemi," Allatin explained. "We dare not put in there, or at any other inhabited place. A ways down there are a couple of big islands offshore—we will want to avoid those as well. But in between is a fair stretch of uninhabited shoreline. We'll make for there. We should be able to leave the *Restless Heart* offshore there for days without her being seen."

"I think you should move her about," Gorian suggested. "Don't let her just sit there. Someone might happen by."

"Agreed," Kral said, not entirely sure why they had called him over.

Gorian answered that quickly enough, though. "We still are not sure what you lot are after in Stygia, Kral," he said. "We have reason to believe that we are not too far from our own goal here, but we know not where exactly you want to go."

"Nor will I tell you," Kral said. "But the truth is, I am not yet sure exactly where I need to go either. You get me to Stygia, and I'll worry about the rest."

In the moonlight, Kral could see that Allatin was uncomfortable with his answer. But Gorian just nodded. "Fine," he said. "You have not asked my business, and I can but do you the same courtesy. You will be alerted when we are about to drop anchor, and we will take the remaining boat over to shore or swim there. You can stay with us as long as you like, or split off at any time."

"Very well," Kral said. He tried to display no emotion before these men, but inside he was nearly bursting with anticipation. What he had told them was true—he had no idea where in Stygia to look for the crown. A clue would present itself, he was sure, even if he had to turn the country upside down to find it. In the meantime, traveling with Gorian and his mercenaries would be safer than striking out completely on their own in unfamiliar and unfriendly territory.

He excused himself and went to tell the others the news.

Entering the cabin, he found them crowded around the porthole, watching the lights of Khemi skate by.

"That's Khemi, isn't it?" Mikelo said, when Kral closed the door.

"Yes."

"I told you!" Mikelo exclaimed.

"My first view of Stygia, and I can see nothing," Donial said.

"Which is as much as you want to see," Mikelo offered. "Trust me. There is nothing there but sand and snakes and sorcery."

Alanya shuddered visibly in the moonlight streaming

in through the porthole. "I care little for snakes. Or sorcery."

"Sorcery is responsible for our being here," Kral pointed out. "If not for Gorian's magic . . ."

"I know," she said. "But I still don't like it."

"I hate snakes," Mikelo said, making a face. Revulsion was evident in his voice as well. "Snakes are the worst."

"I've never minded snakes," Donial said.

"You've never seen snakes such as they have in Stygia," Mikelo reminded him. "They grow them huge here and make no attempt to control them. It is an awful thing."

Kral had heard the same thing in stories. "With any luck, we search for a man, not a snake. I doubt that any snake has stolen my people's crown."

"In any other place, I would agree with you," Mikelo put in. "But here . . . it could be either. Or both, working in concert." He shivered, wrapped his arms around his skinny frame. "Snakes. Brrr!"

THE NEXT HOUR found the group assembled on the deck, preparing to venture into night-shrouded Stygia. It had been decided that Alanya, the only female, and Mikelo, the youngest, would go over in the boat along with a single mercenary to help row and all the supplies, weapons, and so on that would be needed on shore. Donial didn't mind swimming, and it was obvious, from the gear the mercenaries loaded onto the small craft, that they expected serious trouble.

The little boat pushed away from the *Restless Heart,* and the rest of the men dove into the water to swim with it. A single mercenary remained on board with the *Heart* sailors, to make sure they didn't just abandon those on the shore. If the ship was spotted, they were to take evasive actions, then return to the same place two nights later to check for the onshore party. Donial watched the boat cast off, then the mercenaries splashing into the sea around it. He stood on the deck with Kral, who tossed him a relaxed grin and a nod. Together, they dove over the side.

Donial had no fear of getting lost in this sea. The water was relatively calm, and the mercenaries all swam around the boat, headed for the dark patch of shoreline ahead. He had taken Mikelo's warnings about snakes to heart and wondered if there were water snakes in the shallows. But the sheer number of swimmers and the thunder their progress made in the water would doubtless scare away any aquatic predators.

During the swim, Donial wondered what they would find in Stygia. He knew what Kral was after, but didn't know how the Pict could expect to find it in such a vast and secretive country. So far, since leaving Tarantia, they had experienced nothing but danger and disappointment. The battle against the Argossean pirates had promised excitement, at first. It proved bloody and horrifying, instead. Donial had—with his sister's aid—killed a man. His first killing. There had been nothing glamorous or exciting about it. Instead it was brutal, ugly. When the task was done, Donial had felt sick. He had wanted to rush down to the water and bathe in it, as if he could cleanse the action from his memory.

That had been followed by days of captivity. Never knowing which day would be his last, when the pirate captain might decide his hostages were useless after all. The anxiety of attempted escape had added to his discomfort. Finally, with magical assistance from the mercenary leader Gorian, the surviving sailors and mercenaries rose up against Kunios and his buccaneers, regaining the *Restless Heart* and leaving the Argosseans stranded on the coast of Shem. They had set sail for Stygia, which should have been cause for rejoicing. But Donial didn't feel like a celebration. What was ahead seemed at least as hard as that which lay behind them.

Somehow, for the most part Alanya kept her spirits up. She was not the carefree girl she had been before their time in Koronaka, but she didn't seem to take the frustrations to heart, as he did. Everything they had experienced had matured both of them, he suspected. But he was finding it ever more difficult to pretend to be happy and carefree. He could not remember the last time he had actually laughed out loud.

Donial had been anxious for his childhood to be over. To be treated as an adult instead of a little kid. Now, undeniably, it was.

He couldn't help wishing maybe it had lasted a little longer.

Almost before he knew it, he could feel sandy ocean bottom under his feet. He waded the rest of the way ashore, surrounded by the others. Moonlight washed the strip of beach he emerged onto, seawater running off him. Beyond the beach, he could see only more sand, broken by occasional dark clots that he assumed were bushes or low, stunted trees. Desert ran right to the ocean's edge.

The view, such as it was, matched Donial's mood. Dark, and without much promise.

He located Alanya and Mikelo, then Kral joined them. The four companions walked over to the edge of the group, where they could speak privately. "What now?" Donial asked. "Where do we go?"

"I am still not sure," Kral answered, his voice low. "But I have an idea."

"What is it?" Alanya wondered.

"Look at what we know of Gorian and his soldiers," he replied. "They came here from Tarantia, at the same time as we did and with the same sense of urgency. They are in league with a magician back in Tarantia. They seek something here in Stygia and expect to have to fight for it. All these things make me believe that their goal is the same as ours."

"They are after the crown?" Donial asked, surprised.

"I think they may be," Kral said. "We know that some Stygian mage had it stolen from the thief who took it from your uncle. Lupinius was trying to sell it, so he would not have kept its existence a secret. We know, also, that numerous parties were aware of it, probably including those strangers we saw creeping away from your father's home the night we found Lupinius wounded. We assumed that the thief who took the Teeth stabbed him and killed the Ranger, but it could as easily have been those men, who were empty-handed when they left. My thinking is that those men included Gorian, or someone working with him. Probably trying to find the Teeth on behalf of the sorcerer who gave him that magic stone he wears around his neck."

"You make many assumptions, Kral," Alanya pointed out.

"Yes, Alanya," he said. "But the facts are the facts. How would a Stygian sorcerer have known the whereabouts of the Teeth in Tarantia? He must have heard about it from someone. There had not been time to send a message by any of the usual means, and then for those priests to have arrived to take the crown from Tremont. But one wizard to another might have been able to do it—they have ways of communicating that we cannot comprehend. If there are mages competing for the Teeth, is it not reasonable to expect that the Aquilonian one might have sent an armed force after it, once the Stygians had taken it?"

Donial listened to Kral's theory with disbelief. Had they spent all this time at sea with people who were after the same thing they were—and would fight to keep it? But the more he considered Kral's words, the more he realized that they made sense. Surely there could have been some other reason for Gorian's hasty journey to Stygia. But any other reason would be almost too coincidental to be believed. Given the timing, and the nature of the expedition—especially, as Kral pointed out, the connection to some unknown Aquilonian mage—the obvious answer was most likely the correct one.

Gorian and his men were here for the Teeth of the Ice Bear. And, since they had the assistance of some sorcerer—who had presumably told the Stygian responsible for its theft about the crown in the first place—they would have some idea where to find it.

Not much to go on, he knew. But better than nothing, which was what they had had only moments before.

"So we stay with them?" Mikelo asked, just as Donial was about to.

"Yes," Kral replied. "And when they find the crown, we take it instead."

"There are more of them, and better armed," Donial said. "And they have magic on their side."

Kral chuckled, without humor. "Did I say it would be easy?"

3

KUTHMET WAS A day's hike from the coast where they had landed. The sun blazed down on the little party, making Kral glad he was not, like the mercenaries, burdened by a shirt of mail, a helmet, and a shield in addition to his weapons. Though the sun of his Pictish homeland was rarely so hot, his flesh was still accustomed to its rays.

With no time to lose, they had to take the chance of walking during the day. This was an unpopulated part of Stygia, the bulk of the nation's people having made their homes in cities along the River Styx, where water was plentiful. Here there was nothing but buff-colored desert cut by low ridges of rock. Scrubby pale plants erupted from the dry ground here and there, most bearing thorns or long, spiky leaves. A few birds, primarily vultures, wheeled about in the cloudless sky. Lizards and small snakes sunned themselves on rocks or scuttled away at the approach of the group.

Everyone carried as much water in skins and bladders as they could handle, since no one knew if there were oases between here and Kuthmet. Even if there were, those were the likeliest spots to run into Stygians, which they hoped to avoid.

As they walked, Kral tried to subtly interrogate one of the mercenaries, a Corinthian named Galados. The man was leaner than most of the others, with a more cultured air than Kral expected from mercenaries. Or at least it seemed that way to him, although being a Pict, he realized he could have been mistaken about that part. The man seemed curious about him, though, and had asked him questions from time to time about Pictish customs and beliefs. He allowed Galados to begin the conversation now, answering a couple of questions about his clan's hunting practices, then tried to turn the subject around.

"How do you know that whatever you seek is in Kuthmet?" he asked. "Stygia is a big place, is it not?"

"That it is," Galados replied. "But as for how we know, I go where I am told. Gorian is the one who pays me, so Gorian decides my destination."

"Then Gorian is the man behind your whole expedition? Or does he represent someone else?"

Galados smoothed down his brown mustache. He also wore a neatly trimmed, wedge-shaped beard. His eyes turned down slightly at the outside corners, giving him a sense of perpetual sadness. "He has a sponsor," he said after a moment's pause. "A magician of some sort, I'd wager. I know the man not at all, and saw him but once, ere we left Tarantia."

"So you are all in search of some object that a magician would value," Kral pressed.

"I am in search of the coins that Gorian agreed to pay, when the task is done," Galados answered. "No less and no more."

Kral could tell that the man had answered all the questions about their mission that he was going to. But he had heard enough to confirm his suspicions. An Aquilonian mage was behind Gorian's quest.

It had to be the Teeth, then. No other explanation made sense.

Before the Corinthian could question him further, Kral rejoined his friends. "They are definitely after the Teeth," he said when he reached them. In hushed tones, he explained his reasoning.

"How long will they let us stay with them?" Mikelo asked.

"I know not," Kral said. "But until they force us away we should stay close and try to learn whatever we can about their destination. Having narrowed it to Kuthmet is good. But this lot knows more than that, and if there is a way we can find out what they know, then the Teeth is as good as ours."

"I will try," Mikelo offered. "They know that we have become friendly, these last several days. But they also know that before the Argosseans attacked your party, you knew me not. Perhaps I can persuade them that I would rather join their quest than yours."

"That could be dangerous, Mikelo," Donial observed. "If you are found out."

"I know," Mikelo replied. "But I see no better way to learn what they know."

Alanya considered for a moment. "It might be more believable if you had an argument with us. Some reason to want to leave our group and join theirs."

"That makes sense," Mikelo said. "About what?"

Alanya made a pondering face, but inspiration struck Kral. "Stop staring at her!" he shouted. He realized as he did that some of the anger he feigned was real—Mikelo did have a habit of gazing longingly at Alanya, and Kral found it annoying in the extreme. "You're always staring at her, and she doesn't like it!"

Donial broke into a huge grin as he realized what Kral had started. "That's right!" he added loudly. "My sister is sick of you, so just leave her alone!"

Mikelo's face collapsed. Kral thought the young Zingaran was about to cry. He still had not caught on. Perhaps it was the genuine emotion that Kral and Donial were expressing, or maybe the whole thing simply felt too real to him. Maybe he even thought the attention he had been paying to Alanya had gone unnoticed, until now.

If that was the case, he was sadly deluded. Kral had not spoken with Alanya about it, but he and Donial were both aware of Mikelo's feelings for her and had talked about it between themselves. He could not have been more obvious if he had tied himself to her with a scarlet sash.

"Alanya will never love you," Kral put in. "So you might as well give up."

Alanya had stopped dead, dumfounded. But as she watched the others, a sly smile crept across her lovely face. "Mikelo," she said in a low whisper. "This is the fight you need. But you need to respond as well."

Mikelo's visage noticeably brightened. Kral could see that he finally understood. "Well and good!" he shouted back. "If she truly feels that way, then I want nothing to do with her!" He balled his hands into fists and stomped on the ground in a fashion that Kral found overly dramatic. He hoped onlookers—for some of the mercenaries were watching now—did not realize he was performing for their benefit.

After a few moments of glaring at the others, Mikelo stormed away. Kral, Alanya, and Donial watched him go, then turned back to one another, shrugging and pretending to make small talk. They could hear Mikelo ranting to the mercenaries when he reached them, but not what he said.

What he said mattered little. The important thing was that the plan had been hatched and put into place in a very few minutes. Which was good, as they were advancing toward Kuthmet, and there were precious few minutes to spare.

THE MERCENARY CREW stopped that night on a low crest of rock that looked out toward the lights of Kuthmet. The nature of the desert they traversed over the course of the day had changed. The ground had become deep sand that shifted and blew in the ever-present winds. Gorian didn't like it. The sand stung when it blew at him, particularly since his skin had been dried out and burned by the heat of the sun. With the fall of night, however, the wind had died, and the temperature dropped with it.

Now he hunkered down on the ridge looking out toward Kuthmet. Somewhere down there was the crown that Kanilla Rey wanted. He hoped they could achieve their goal. The nineteen soldiers he'd started with had been winnowed down to eight, plus himself and Sullas. And one of those eight, Elonius, was back on the *Restless Heart* to make sure the sailors didn't just take off and leave them stranded here.

He had seen those damnable Stygians at work once, and knew that the whole force of twenty would have had a hard time defeating them. The only hope would have been for some of the men to rush the wizards while the others were blasted by their mystical ways. Or course, it was possible that Kanilla Rey could help, even over this distance, as he had with the pirates back in Shem.

Still, twenty would have been better. An army, better still.

The other unknown was the young people, the strange trio of the Pict and his two Aquilonian friends. They had never given any indication of why they had come to Stygia. The longer they traveled with his group, the more he wondered if they were after the same thing.

After all, the crown had Pictish origins, it was said. That in itself had raised his suspicions from the start. But the Pict in particular had proven useful from time to time, so as long as they weren't too near the goal, he had not bothered to do anything about them.

Now, however, they were near the goal. Something would have to be done.

The Pict would be a hard one to kill. The Aquilonians easier, although the ship's boy from the old *Barachan Spur* would likely complain when they went to do the girl. She was a fine-looking one, at that.

Maybe they could just kill the Pict and the brother, and keep her alive. Looking back down the slope, he spotted a Gunderman mercenary named Hakon squatting down and drinking water from a bladder. He called the man's name and beckoned him up the ridge.

"Yes?" Hakon asked when he arrived. He dropped to his haunches next to Gorian. He was a tall man, well over six feet, with muscles like corded steel. His shoulders were wide. A massive two-handed broadsword hung in a scabbard on his back, tied across his huge chest. His light brown hair was trimmed close to his head, and Gorian had seen him shaving his beard with a dagger most mornings, scraping its edge across a prominent jaw. Like all the mercenaries Gorian had hired, he spoke Aquilonian well.

"That Pict boy. What do you think of him?"

Hakon considered the question only briefly. He blinked a couple of times, long, almost feminine lashes fluttering over eyes of a deep cerulean blue. His lips were thin and pale. "A good fighter. I saw him put down what seems like ten of those Argossean dogs, back on that beach in Shem."

"He is that," Gorian agreed. "Anything else?"

"Smart, I think. For a savage. I spent some time on the border, and made a few raids into the Pictish wilderness. I have no love for that kind. I've seen what they do— taking heads, boiling the skin off, and piling the skulls in their villages like some kind of . . . mementos, I guess. And you would not want to be a woman in that land, I can tell you. But most of the Picts I encountered—not that they lived to have conversation with—seemed little more than forest beasts to me. Might as well have been wolves as men. This one—he's different. Not just that he's friends with those two Aquilonians. I have heard him speak, and he uses the language well. Not like a native. But nearly as well as I. And more than that. He seems to be thinking, all the time. I know not what about. But there is intelligence in his eyes, not the animal dullness I would expect there."

Gorian nodded. He had reached similar conclusions about the Pict. But he knew what the Gunderman didn't—that there was a probable connection between the boy and the prize they sought.

"Can you kill him?"

Hakon's unexpectedly blue eyes widened in surprise. "I am right here next to you. Many have tried to kill me. They are dead. Not me."

"You yourself said he was good, and smart."

"I am better," Hakon said. "Without question."

"Very well," Gorian said. That was the answer he had wanted to hear. He was glad, too, of the confidence in Hakon's voice.

"When do you want it done?" Hakon asked.

He had not decided yet. There was still time—they weren't moving on Kuthmet until the next night. If they tried tonight, after walking all day, they would not be at their best. And to go up against those Stygians they would need to be. They would camp here, just out of sight of the city. Restore their energy. Then when darkness fell again, they would move.

"I will tell you when," he said. "Just be ready, on my word."

"Worry not, Gorian. When the time comes, I will do it, and happily. As soon as I saw we had a Pict on the ship with us, I wanted to do it then. I hate them. Every last one of them."

Gorian promised that Hakon would get the chance, then dismissed the man so he could get back to planning their next move. He had found out from Kanilla Rey that their target was a sorcerer named Shehkmi al Nasir. The men who had taken the crown had been acolytes of his. He had many followers, it seemed, in Kuthmet, where he was regarded as powerful, a force to be feared.

Well, Gorian had seen that, firsthand. He was already afraid of Shehkmi al Nasir, and he had not even met the wizard yet. But he would do his master's bidding, no matter what. He was Kanilla Rey's man. He did what he was told.

4

"LET'S GO!"

Alanya woke suddenly, startled by Mikelo's hand on her shoulder and his urgent whisper in her ear.

"What is it?" she demanded.

"We should leave," Mikelo said. He turned away from her, shook Donial awake. Kral was already sitting up. It was still night. A sliver of moon floated just above the horizon.

"What have you learned?" Kral asked. As usual, Alanya thought, he was alert immediately upon awakening. It still took her a minute to get her bearings, and she had not remembered at first that they had feigned the fight with Mikelo so that he could get information from the mercenaries.

"Come on," Mikelo urged. "We should get away from here quickly. I can tell you on the way."

Alanya shrugged off the cloak that had covered her. "Very well," she said. "I am ready." She got to her feet, glancing toward the nearby slope where the mercenaries slept. So far, none of them seemed to be looking their way. She kept expecting someone to notice them, to come running, as had happened when the same group of four had tried to escape the pirates in much the same fashion. But the pirates had not wanted them to leave; these mercenaries probably didn't care one way or the other.

Within moments, the others had gathered their things. Except for the clothes he wore, Mikelo had nothing but a sword and a couple of knives, affixed to his belt. They moved out as silently as they could, finding their way by the moon's faint glow toward the distant lights of Kuthmet.

When they were a comfortable distance away from the mercenaries, Mikelo said, "The men were talking about a magician named Shehkmi al Nasir. That's who Gorian said they would be looking for."

"So this magician has the crown," Kral speculated.

"Or will soon," Donial said. "That storm that blew us off course might well have done the same to the Stygians."

"It's possible," Kral agreed. "We were delayed many days by fixing the *Restless Heart,* but they may have been equally delayed. Assuming he already has it is probably our safest course, though."

"Aye," Mikelo said. "My thought as well. The soldiers

seemed to think he did. Their plan is to rest tonight and tomorrow, then to attack his home tomorrow night."

"That leaves little time for us to locate him," Donial pointed out.

"But locate him we shall," Kral said. "Getting the crown back is too important not to. And we cannot let Gorian and his crew get their hands on it."

"Kral," Alanya said, an idea occurring to her on the spot. "If he means to take it back to Aquilonia, to deliver it to some sponsor there, why not let him? Would it not be just as easy to let them carry it back to Tarantia for us, then take it from them once they get there?"

Kral shook his head. "I had thought of that," he admitted. "But I know not who in Aquilonia Gorian works for. What if it is a more powerful mage than this al Nasir? What if there are a hundred soldiers in Tarantia to guard it instead of a handful? Besides, if we can get the Teeth now, we can take the *Restless Heart* and sail all the way around to the western edge of the Pictish lands. It will save time and be safer than going overland, back through Aquilonia."

She remembered that Kral was a wanted man in Tarantia, still suspected of murder, and that he had escaped from an Aquilonian prison. He would probably be happiest never to have to set foot in Tarantia again, or in any of the lands ruled by King Conan.

"That makes sense," she said, easily accepting his reasoning. "If we can take the *Restless Heart*."

"We can take it," Kral said. He sounded utterly confident of his ability to do just that.

They walked along in silence for a while. Overhead, the sky grew more gray. As sunrise neared, the wind began to pick up again. Alanya was trudging along, head down to keep windblown sand out of her eyes, when Mikelo sidled up next to her.

"What they said earlier?" he began. "About me . . . you know, watching you."

"Yes?" Alanya said. She didn't know where he intended to take the conversation, but was uncomfortable with just about any direction it might lead.

"I think . . . I think they were right," he stammered. "It . . . it is difficult for me to admit it to you, but I . . . I do consider you a very beautiful woman. Never do I remember seeing another such as you. I cannot help but stare whenever my gaze falls upon you. If this displeases you or causes you discomfort, then I apologize, but my will is not my own in such matters. If I thought that you would have me, I would ask for your hand now, our ages and circumstances be damned."

Alanya kept walking, trying not to laugh, because Mikelo was clearly so serious, even solemn, about what he confessed. She would not take him as a husband, now or ever. She was sure about that. He was a perfectly nice boy. But that was all he was, and that was how she suspected she would always see him. A boy, not a man. Certainly not a vigorous, vital man like Kral.

He had admitted that it was hard for him to say, and she had no doubt that it had been. Probably also something he could not bring himself not to say, once Kral had started the argument about it. "I . . . appreciate what you say," she managed. "And I like you, Mikelo. But I am not interested in being betrothed. To you, or anybody. I hope you can understand that."

"Of course." Mikelo sounded morose, but she could not see his expression. He had probably brought up the topic just now for that exact reason, knowing that the blinding sand would make it hard for her to watch his face.

"Did the men give up the information about Shehkmi al Nasir easily?" she asked, hoping to push the discussion onto less uncomfortable ground. "Did they trust you after they overheard our fight?"

"Not at all," Mikelo replied. He gave a chuckle, sounding relieved that Alanya had not taken offense at his advance. "No one wanted to tell me anything. But they talked among themselves, and after some time, they stopped working so hard at trying to prevent me from hearing."

"And you are sure about the name?"

"I am as sure of it as I am that the sun is rising, and with it the wind," he said. As he spoke, he batted at sand as if he could knock it away with his hand. "I feel like I will be tasting sand for the rest of my life."

Depending on how powerful this sorcerer is, you might, Alanya thought. But she held her tongue. In fact, the wind blew harder, and she pressed her lips tightly together, closing her eyes but for tiny slits to see through. Sand lashed at her, stinging like the tails of thousands of tiny whips. She felt Kral's presence beside her, and realized he was moving out in front to block some of the worst of it with his body. She would have said something about it, told him not to bother, but the steady hum of the wind had escalated to something like constant thunder. To speak would have required shouting, and she did not want her mouth open that wide.

So she kept her mouth shut. Kral's efforts were for naught; the wind blew too hard, the sand flew everywhere. She felt it caking the corners of her eyes and mouth, felt it snaking beneath her clothing. Head down, buffeted now by the wind, she walked on. It pushed at her, tried to knock her down. Kral leaned into it and Alanya did the same. Her hair broke free of the band that held it together and flew unrestrained. The cloak across her shoulders fluttered and snapped like the sails of the *Restless Heart* during the storm that had nearly torn the ship apart. The blue of the sky had disappeared, shrouded by sand.

She was vaguely aware of sudden motion up ahead. She dared to lift her head, to peer through her slitted eyes. Kral was running toward Donial, who had wandered farther from the others than was safe in this— already, she could barely make him out. She glanced to her right to make sure that Mikelo was still there. Having retrieved Alanya's brother, Kral drew him back toward the other two. He motioned for them to stop where they were.

"The storm is getting worse!" he shouted when he reached them. "We cannot keep going in this! We need to wait and let it blow over!"

Alanya nodded her assent. She saw Kral straighten

and look about, and a moment later he gestured them all toward a wispy bush, blown almost sideways by the wind. "It will not provide much shelter!" he called. "But better than none at all!"

He led the way over to the little scrap of brush and dropped to his haunches behind it. The others did likewise. At Kral's signal, they moved about until they formed a kind of circle, facing each other, backs out. They wrapped cloaks about themselves as best they could. Still, sand bit and insinuated and scoured, but not quite as bad as before. Alanya wondered how long it could last. Every minute they sat here was another minute they would not have to find the Teeth of the Ice Bear before Gorian and his men came looking for it.

But the wind showed no sign of letting up.

They waited.

5

GOVERNOR SHARZEN OF Koronaka heard the drums even in his sleep. He would have sworn that they never stopped, never paused, but perhaps they did. Perhaps it was only in his imagination that they went on hour after hour, all through the night, and were still sounding come morning.

Or perhaps not.

Now, standing by his window in the first rays of the sun, the drumming was definitely real. It seemed to fill every valley of the Pictish lands, to echo from every mountain. It sounded as if the forest itself had come to horrible life, trees beating against their own bark-covered chests with branch arms and fists of twigs.

It had started with the dawn, six days before. A persistent, tuneless drumming. Less like music than like random sounds. Scouts had been dispatched into the forests to find out what it meant. First a pair of them, then when they did not return, six more. Then twenty, in groups of four.

None came back.

Sharzen poured himself his first flagon of wine for the morning. Ever since the drums began, he had not been able to start his day without one. And he kept one close at hand until he could finally fall asleep at night.

He had never felt so alone. Not for the first time, he realized that he missed Lupinius. The man had been a scoundrel, out only for himself, as false a friend as any-one could fear to have. But even with all that, he had been a reassuring presence. When one was virtually friendless, isolated by power and position, even a make-believe friend was better than none. Lupinius would have had some idea of how to deal with the inter-minable drumming noise.

Sharzen had had ideas the first day or so, but now the drums rattled him so much that he could barely think straight. When the scouts had failed to return he had been unable to come up with any new thoughts. Instead, he had summoned Gestian, the captain who commanded Koronaka's troops, and told him that the defense of the settlement was in his hands. Gestian had accepted the responsibility without comment. His ranks had been swelled lately, with the addition of many of the Rangers left unemployed by Lupinius's sudden absence. Without funding from Aquilonia, Sharzen was not sure how long he would be able to pay any of the soldiers. But he had sent several urgent messages to King Conan, telling him that the Pictish problem was getting worse, and he needed more support from Tarantia. He had heard that the King was, in fact, taking the situation seriously, and had ordered troops sent to the Westermarck to reinforce the settlements there.

Listening to the drums, Sharzen just hoped it wasn't too little, too late.

WHEN KRAL DARED to move again, his joints were locked, his muscles aching from sitting rigid and motionless against the punishing winds. He was entirely crusted with a coating of sand. He kept his eyes tightly shut and wiped their outer surface, but with hands so sandy he was not sure if it did any good. He was sure the wind had died at last, so he forced himself to look.

The sun was visible again, its rays already beginning to heat the air. Kral's companions were practically indistinguishable from the desert floor itself, so caked with sand were they. Donial had fallen asleep, so Kral shook him gently. Alanya and Mikelo moved under their own power, but they were all sore and stiff.

"How much time do you think we lost?" Alanya asked, blinking in the sun's glare.

"Too much," Kral replied. "We had a good lead on Gorian and we have lost time. Even if the sandstorm hit them, they were staying still today, so it would not have affected their progress."

"Do you think it was a natural storm?" Donial asked,

sounding a bit concerned. "Or was it that Stygian mage's doing?"

"I would say natural," Mikelo answered. "I told you that Stygia was a hellish place. I have heard of such storms lasting a day and a night and another day."

"Even if this Shehkmi al Nasir knows that his Aquilonian rival has sent soldiers for the Teeth," Kral said, "he would have no way to know of our approach."

"But who knows what magicians know, or how?" Donial queried. "They have ways beyond the ken of mere humans."

"Aye," Mikelo agreed. "So I have heard, as well."

"The shamans of my people have their secrets," Kral said. "And inexplicable knowledge is often among them. Still, we are only four, traveling lightly. The mercenaries are twice our number. I would consider them the greater threat"—here he paused, and smiled, aware of his imminent immodesty—"if I did not know us."

The others laughed. Kral had never been one to overstate his own abilities and accomplishments. Some in his clan had done that, and usually they were shown as liars or fools before too long. Kral had learned well from their mistakes and was careful not to make claims for himself that he could not back up with action.

But at the same time, these last weeks he had found that he was capable of much more than he ever expected. With that new self-knowledge came new confidence. He was strong, he was skilled, and he was possessed of an inordinate amount of courage. Perhaps most important, he had whatever quality makes a person a leader instead of a follower—someone other people would gladly put their trust in and risk their lives for. His army was tiny, it was true, but they were loyal and steadfast and would do anything for him.

And he for them. That, he supposed, was the true test of leadership. Making sure one's followers knew that there was a good reason they looked to the leader for direction and example.

Now, he thought, he needed to lead again. Kuthmet, Shehkmi al Nasir, and the Teeth of the Ice Bear waited.

AS THEY NEARED the city, Kral could smell water in the air. He had almost begun to give up hope that he would ever smell that again—the slightly fetid, fishy aroma of a river. The desert was almost odorless, in a way. Nothing but dry air and dirt. One had to be right on top of the few scraggly bushes to smell anything at all from them.

The sun was high overhead when they reached the city's outskirts. The buildings here were low to the ground, the same color as the sand surrounding them, with narrow passageways between. There were no walls around the city of Kuthmet. The city's authorities, Kral supposed, relied on the harsh desert to provide protection from marauders—that, and the Styx forming its northern barrier. And, Kral guessed with a shiver, quite possibly the magic of Shehkmi al Nasir and those like him.

Other smells mingled with the river's odor now. Kral could smell fires burning, food cooking. The scent of

people and animals, masses of them living close together. Sweat and sewage. Oils and soaps. Underneath it
all, another, odd smell. Something he could not identify.

Mikelo saw him wrinkling his nose, trying to figure
it out. "Do you smell that?" Kral asked him.

Mikelo looked worried. "Snakes," he said. "That is
the smell of snakes. And the sun is still up. At night, it
gets much worse."

"Worse in what way?" Donial asked.

"More of them," Mikelo explained. "A lot more."

Kral had little experience with snakes. They were
blessedly rare in the Pictish wilderness. But from what
he had heard, he did not expect to enjoy their company.
"Then maybe we can conclude our business during the
day."

He started down one of the narrow alleyways between the squared-off, low structures. Before he had
gone far, Alanya spoke up. "How do you propose we
find this magician?" she asked.

Kral had given this a lot of thought on the long hike
over, and he had come up with an idea. He had discussed it briefly with Mikelo, who after all had been to
Stygia once before, but hadn't brought it up with the
others yet. "What Mikelo and I were thinking," he said,
"is that almost everyone in town probably knows who
Shehkmi al Nasir is and where he can be found. Many
of the people we might meet would think it in their best
interests to report our presence to him, rather than tell
us where to look. Perhaps most of them. But there might
be a group of people who would care not if something

were to happen to al Nasir and would have very little interest in protecting him."

"Who would that be?" Donial wondered.

"Mikelo says that Stygian sorcerers often use slave labor," Kral replied. "And that if al Nasir is like most he's heard about, he is probably a cruel master. If we can find where his slaves dwell, perhaps we can get some help from them."

"That seems like a good idea," Alanya said. "If we can find them."

"If we went about asking for Shehkmi al Nasir, people would likely take notice of us," Mikelo offered. "But if we ask for his slaves, they will barely recognize our existence."

"Except for one thing," Donial brought up. "Or maybe two. A Pict in Stygia is likely a very odd sight. And the same for a blond girl. I think we need to disguise both of you before we are seen by anyone."

Kral nodded toward one of the nearby buildings. "We could break into a house," he suggested. "Find some clothing more suited to Stygia. We might also find trouble, if someone is inside."

"What about my hair?" Alanya asked.

Kral shrugged. "Maybe we can find something with a hood. Were we in the forest, I would know how to make a black dye, but there is a definite scarcity of trees around here."

"We can look anyway," Alanya said. "There might be something."

Kral was a little hesitant about entering some unknown house here. The neighborhood was quiet—so far, they had not seen a single person. But that didn't mean everyone wasn't inside. He would hate to start their visit to Kuthmet by having to kill a family of locals. Once they were in, however, they were committed—they could not leave witnesses alive to sound an alarm.

His own experience with solid houses was still somewhat limited, so he let the others decide which building to try. The one they picked was, like the rest of its neighbors, square, flat-roofed, with only narrow window slits. A rough wooden door bolted from the outside indicated that whoever lived within had gone out. Kral pressed an ear to the door, listening. He heard nothing from the inside.

"Best get at it," he said softly. "Before someone comes around."

The others murmured assent. He slid back the bolt, pushed the door open. Inside, the house was plain, its raw plank floor partly covered by a woven, patterned rug, a few pieces of wooden furniture standing about. Pots and pans hung on a hearth, and dark ash filled the fireplace. Smells of cooking with rich spices lingered in the air.

"A bedroom," Alanya whispered. "That is where the clothing would be, most likely."

An interior doorway led to another room. Kral passed through and saw a sleeping area with two straw mats on the floor next to a wooden chest. Opening the chest, he found that it was full of folded Stygian clothing—dark

robes, and a few others, some almost white, some a reddish brown with darker patterns. He pawed through them
until he found one big enough to fit him, then passed
smaller ones to the others.

Alanya, meanwhile, was examining another chest,
with clay bottles ranged on top of it. She pulled the
stoppers from some of them, sniffing their contents. A
couple of times she poured a few drops on her hand and
looked at it.

"What are you doing?" Donial asked her.

"I think this is henna dye," she said.

"Can you use it on your hair?"

"I think so. It will make it reddish, not black like a
Stygian woman's. But darker than it is."

"Can you add some of the ash from the fireplace?"
Kral wondered. "Would that make it darker?"

"It will stink," Alanya said. "But I suppose it might."

She poured some of the stuff into her hand, then
went back into the other room. When she returned, rubbing her hands together to mix the ash and dye, Kral,
Donial and Mikelo had all donned their stolen robes.
Kral's had a hood that covered his head. Alanya tossed
him a wan smile. "I am not sure what this will look like,"
she warned. With that, she worked the mixture into her
hair. Almost instantly, it was darker, matted with the
pasty substance.

He gave her a robe to put on over her shift. When she
had fixed it about herself, she looked at him again, her
luxurious hair thick and drooping. Nothing could be

done about her blue eyes, but Kral guessed that if anyone came close enough to see those, he could take care
of it. "Am I beautiful?" she asked teasingly.

"Always," he said.

Not teasing a bit.

6

AS HER HAIR dried, Alanya kept pulling a lock in front of her eyes to check on it. It had indeed turned several shades darker, if not quite the rich, jet-black common to Stygians. She hoped it would hold after she rinsed it out in clean water—if she had the chance to do so—because the combination of henna dye and wood ash stank like . . . well, like nothing she had ever put on her head, that was for sure.

They walked through Kuthmet, toward the center of town. Here, there were plenty of people, busily going about their business or simply sitting in teahouses, smoking pipes and sipping tea from small ceramic cups. A few of them glanced at the quartet, strangers in their town, but for the most part no one paid them any real attention. Alanya credited their disguises. Somehow, she felt like the dark hair made her a different person: mysterious, exotic, a young lady with no history, no past. She liked the feeling.

Once in a while they stopped so Mikelo could ask someone, as discreetly as possible, where the slave classes might be found. A Stygian woman directed them to a neighborhood on the city's eastern fringe. The four passed through the center of town, not talking much lest their voices and language give them away, keeping their eyes on the ground. When they saw acolytes of Set, recognizable because of their flowing black robes and shaved heads, they stepped to the side of the road or went to a different street altogether. Others did the same, and Alanya had a definite sense that people lived in a perpetual state of fear in this city.

They had been inside the city for a couple of hours when they made it to the slave area. Here the buildings were smaller, more run-down, the streets closer together and more crowded. The smells of cooking were more pronounced and pungent than they had been in the rest of Kuthmet. Skins tended to be darker, as well, as most of the slaves here were from the south, Kush or Darfar or the Black Kingdoms. Most, though by no means all—Alanya also saw people who looked to her like Khaurans and Zamorans, Vendhyans, even a few who might have been Aquilonian. She even saw a couple of blondes, and touched her own hair, remembering how it used to look. And smell.

Here, most people were not as fearful or shy. She and her friends were met with direct looks, even stares, and some they encountered even greeted them. One of these, Mikelo replied to, and then after a brief and friendly exchange, he asked a question in Stygian. The response he got seemed animated and affirmative. After, he turned to the others. "We are in luck," he said. "This fellow says he can take us to the home of some of al Nasir's slaves."

"I should have thought they would live with al Nasir," Donial said.

"Often an important Stygian will let his slaves live outside his own premises," Mikelo explained. "Knowing that they will show up as needed. Where are they going to run—off into the desert?"

The dark-skinned man smiled amiably and led the four through a warren of cramped, narrow streets. Alanya began to feel a bit nervous. She had no way to know how bad Mikelo's Stygian was, or what he had really asked their guide. For all she knew, he truly was mad at her and the others and was leading them into some kind of trap. She didn't think that was the case, but the more the streets twisted and turned, so she didn't know if she would ever be able to find her way out, the more she worried. She thought that now she understood how Kral might have felt upon first arriving in Tarantia.

But a few minutes later, the black man pointed them to a particular house. The door was painted a bright flame red and set into a thick mud wall. The man said something Alanya could not understand, then he backed away from them, still smiling and chuckling happily.

"He says this is the home of Tarawa," Mikelo said. "One of al Nasir's most beloved slaves."

"Shouldn't we find one a bit less beloved?" Donial wondered.

"Just because this Tarawa is beloved of al Nasir," Kral countered, "doesn't mean the feeling is returned."

"That was the impression he gave me," Mikelo said. "My Stygian is not the best, I admit. But it didn't sound like Tarawa wasted any love on al Nasir."

"Then let us waste no more time," Kral said. He glanced at the sky, which was already growing grayish blue with the approach of dusk. He went to the door, found a pull-cord beside it, and tugged. From inside they could hear the clang of a bell. A few moments passed, then the door opened.

If this was Tarawa, Alanya could see at a glance why she was a favorite of the sorcerer. The woman at the door was slender and well formed, with a lush, feminine figure. Her skin was nut brown and looked smooth as silk. Thick dark hair fell to the middle of her back. She looked about Alanya's age. Maybe a couple of years older, but no more.

Mikelo said something to her. Alanya caught the name "Tarawa."

The girl smiled. "Yes," she said in good Aquilonian. "I am Tarawa. I imagine you are more comfortable with Aquilonian than Stygian."

"We are," Alanya said. "My name is Alanya. This is my brother Donial, and our friends Kral and Mikelo."

"Welcome," Tarawa said. A quizzical look crossed her face. "You are a long way from home. How is it you happen to be at my door?"

"We were directed here by one we met in the street,"

Kral replied. "He said that you belong to a magician called Shehkmi al Nasir. I am sorry to be so direct, but I fear time is of the essence."

"You are not Aquilonian," Tarawa observed. "My father spent several months in Numalia, and he never described one like you."

"He is a Pict," Alanya explained. "But we have come far, for a very important purpose. Is it true that you serve Shehkmi al Nasir?"

Tarawa laughed. Alanya found herself smiling along with the woman's infectious laughter. "He likes to believe so," Tarawa said. "I was sold to him, at any rate, after being captured by slavers in my native Kush."

"May we come inside?" Alanya asked, still wary of being seen by someone who might mention their presence to the sorcerer.

"Of course." Tarawa stepped out of the doorway to let them pass. Her home was small, a single room with a fireplace and a large pot, a sleeping area, a few wooden chairs, and a table on which rested brightly painted ceramic bowls and dishware.

"Do you live here alone?" Alanya asked her.

"With a few other slaves," Tarawa replied. "Shehkmi al Nasir owns the house. The others are at al Nasir's even now."

"Is he a kind man?"

Tarawa laughed again, but this time without humor. "He is as vicious as a snake," she said. "Without heart or pity or love for anything or anyone. He exists solely for power, for what he can do to become ever stronger.

I doubt that the idea of being kind has ever occurred to him. Certainly he was not kind when he slew my mother, or my brother. I am all that remains of the family."

Once again, Kral let his impatience dictate his next statement. "He has something that belongs to my people. Something very precious to us. I know not what it might mean to him, but it belongs to the Picts. I mean to have it back. Will you help me?"

A look of surprise crossed Tarawa's beautiful face. "My, but you are bold. You think to take something from Shehkmi al Nasir? He is—as he is so fond of reminding everyone—second only to Thoth Amon himself in his sorcerous abilities. Or at least, so he claims—I know not if he speaks the truth. And you—the four of you—believe you can cross him and survive?"

Kral simply shrugged and stared at her. Alanya had seen that look in his eyes before. It said, "Since I have not tried and failed, I have no doubt that I can succeed." It was an attitude she admired a great deal even though she knew at some point he would have to be proven wrong.

But she could not shake a nagging feeling that this was all happening too easily. "How do you suppose it is that the first person we asked brought us right to you, Tarawa?"

Tarawa flashed that beautiful smile at her. "If you asked in the slave district," she said, "it would have been more unusual for you *not* to have been brought to this house. You do not look like people who have come in order to pay tribute to Shehkmi al Nasir. He is much feared in this quarter, and there is no devotion to him except that achieved through whip and blade. Everyone knows that my family and I all serve him, and that I am one of his favorites—though, as I have indicated, the feeling is not returned. So you would naturally have been brought to me, and gladly, by any of the slaves you asked."

The explanation eased Alanya's worries a little. Still, her father had occasionally said, "If something comes to you too easily, it will just be harder later on."

As if reading her mind, Donial asked, "So you will help us?"

"Do you mean to do him any harm?"

"Would it matter if we did?" Kral asked.

Tarawa hesitated, rubbing a prominent cheekbone with her right index finger. "Not necessarily," she answered. "I just want to know what I'm agreeing to before I do."

"We do not plan to hurt him," Kral said. "But I will do whatever is necessary to get my people's crown back."

"Oh, the crown? That's what you seek?"

"You've seen it?" Kral inquired, excited.

"No. No one has, yet. But I have heard it discussed. Al Nasir's acolytes have arrived here in Kuthmet with it, and they plan to present it to him in a ceremony this very night."

"Then there is no time to waste," Kral said. "If we can get it away before he gets his hands on it, so much the better."

Tarawa glanced toward one of the windows. Outside,

the sky was a deep indigo, shading toward black. "Better, indeed. But night falls. It is not a safe time to be on the streets."

"Safety is not my chief concern," Kral said. "The crown is."

"But Kral, the snakes . . ." Mikelo put in.

"Yes, the snakes," Tarawa agreed.

Kral remembered the strange smell he had noticed earlier. Still, what harm could a few snakes do anyone? "No matter the snakes," he insisted. "I will go alone, if need be."

Alanya shook her head. "We will accompany you, Kral," she promised.

"As will I," Tarawa said. "You would never survive in al Nasir's temple without my help."

"Very well, then," Kral said. "Gather whatever you need, Tarawa. As for us, we're ready to face whatever waits out there."

"Or so you think," Tarawa said. Alanya didn't like the look on her face, a look of concern, close to terror. Didn't like it a bit.

7

THE ATTACK CAME at dusk. Sharzen was not expecting it. He thought that when it happened, it would be a morning attack—never dreamed the Picts would begin a battle as night shrouded the settlement of Koronaka. So, while he had never really relaxed since the drumming began, when the day drew to a close he was as close to relaxed as he was likely to get.

Then suddenly the drums stopped pounding. Virtually at the same moment, a piercing scream ripped the evening gloom. Sharzen ran outside. By torchlight, he saw one of his soldiers on the ground below the wall's parapet, an arrow in his gullet. Other soldiers were already running about in response, filling the gap in the wall left by their fallen comrade and preparing to return fire.

"I can't see a blasted thing out there!" Sharzen heard one cry. "It's pitch-black in those woods!"

The only response was an arrow that whistled through the dark and slammed through his helm. The soldier spun around on one foot, then he, too, dropped from the parapet. Sharzen was about to call out an order when there was a noise almost like an oncoming flood, and then the air was full of arrows, thick as gnats in the summer. He ducked back into the relative safety of his mansion's arched doorway. Arrows clattered off the walls, bounced on flagstones, stuck quivering in dirt.

They seemed to come from every direction. Soldiers fell right and left, some screaming out horrible death cries, others dropping silently in instantaneous death.

"To arms!" Sharzen managed to shout. "Fill your hands, men, the Picts are upon us!"

Even as he screamed, he saw Gestian running toward the wall, tugging on his helmet as he did. The captain had a shield strapped to his left arm and a broadsword clapping against his hip as he scurried. The expression on his mustached face was a bit more frantic than Sharzen liked seeing on the commander of Koronaka's troops.

He knew that standing here, even protected by the arch over his doorway, he was in danger. He should go inside, don some armor. Or just stay in, defended by his guards. But his men seemed to have abandoned their posts—they were probably on the wall, or on the way to it, each one assuming that other guards would take care of his safety.

Or, he thought, looking about him at the carnage that had already occurred, they were dead, victims of the earliest arrow volleys that had hit the courtyard.

He went inside the residence, slamming the door against the awful sounds from without.

GESTIAN HAD BEEN on the wall since daybreak. He had spent the day encouraging the men, cajoling them, persuading them to ignore the infernal drumming and keep their eyes on the trees, alert for any potential trouble. He had been moving all day long, from one group of soldiers to the next. Finally, as the sun dipped below the western tree line, he had retired to his quarters and removed his armor. A young woman named Malina would come by in a short while to massage his aching muscles.

He was waiting for her when he heard the first scream, followed by shouts of alarm and a volley of Pictish arrows raining down into the fort. With an angry curse he had grabbed his armor and strapped it back on as quickly as he could, then buckled his sword belt around his middle and dashed back out to the wall.

What he found was a catastrophe.

His troops had taken dozens of casualties, without— as far as he could tell from here—dealing any serious blows in return. The Picts seemed to have the fort surrounded. Arrows flew from every direction. Beyond the walls, the drumming had stopped but now he heard Pictish war cries and other strange noises: birdcalls, animal growls, and so on. He assumed the Picts were using these sounds to communicate. Some kind of code.

He raced across the eastern parapet in a stooped crouch and stopped beside a lieutenant named Alignon. "What news?" he asked, panting for breath from his desperate run.

"I never imagined they would attack at night," Alignon said. "Or even dusk. In my experience, they always make major assaults in the morning."

Gestian risked a peek over the wall. In the shadowed forest he thought he saw a pair of dark eyes regarding him from a blue-tinted face. Before he could really focus on it, however, it vanished into the woods. "I never imagined they would band together to attack us," he said in return.

"You think the Picts have united?"

"The Bear Clan would never have been able to mount an offense like this one," Gestian pointed out. "I doubt any other individual clan would either. No, there are too many of them now—you can see it just by the sheer number of arrows they have sent our way. This is a united effort."

Alignon shivered. "I wonder how many they have."

"Pray to Mitra we never find out."

CONOR WAS ALMOST home to Cimmeria, but the journey wasn't working out quite as he had planned. He had hoped to sell the bizarrely huge teeth along the way, as he was certain they would bring a much better price in Aquilonia than at home in Taern. But while many of the people he showed them to remarked upon their immense size and unusual appearance, no one had any interest in buying loose animal teeth, however large. Conor had threatened a couple of them, to no avail, and had resorted to robbing others of what treasure they did have. In this fashion, he financed his meals and lodging for the nights.

He had traveled virtually due north from Tarantia, to avoid the Border Kingdom. The fewer borders he had to cross, the better he liked it. There were likely to be brigands along the road, but none more ferocious than he. Now he believed he was about two days' journey from Cimmeria if his stolen horse held up. The horse was currently stabled in back of an inn, and Conor was parked inside it, sitting at a table with most of a meal inside him and a few drinks in there with it.

Seated at the table next to his was a traveler who, Conor guessed, had far more wealth than he did. He based this speculation on the man's clothing—blue silks and red satins were prevalent; impractical for the road but attention-grabbing just the same. The man had a thick body and a pudgy, florid face, with bright orange hair like a Vanirman's, only cut shorter. Anyone could see at a glance that he was a civilized man, not one of those northern rogues. *A Nordheim winter would probably kill this one,* Conor thought.

But that didn't mean he might not be interested in parting with some of his gold in exchange for rare and unusual teeth. Conor had struck up a conversation shortly after the man had sat down. Now that he was nearly done, he leaned over to the fellow, who had said his name was Sarapan, of Tauran. "I've something you might be interested in," Conor whispered melodramatically. "If you're the sort of man I think you are."

Sarapan wiped meat gravy from his lips with the back of one hand. "What sort of man is that?" he asked.

"The sort who can appreciate a bargain," Conor said. "Who knows when he sees something of value and is willing to pay a fair price for a sound investment."

"I am a businessman by nature," Sarapan said. He puffed his chest out and picked stray bits of beef from between his teeth. "So I am not surprised you could recognize that quality in me. I admit, however, that I would not have thought of you the same way."

Conor nodded slowly. "I am but a simple barbarian," he said. "Trying to make my way home. This civilized land is not for me. Too many people willing to take advantage of us more simple folk. I can tell that you, though, are too honest for that sort of thing."

Sarapan's face turned even redder. "Yes, honesty is important. Crucial, in my trade. What is it you have?"

"I would rather not show you in here," Conor said. "But if you have a private room . . ."

Of course, the traveler did. Conor had settled for a room shared with three others, one of whom, if judged by odor, might have been a month-dead yak. Sarapan paid for both their meals—part of Conor's plan from the beginning—and they both went upstairs to his private room.

The place was not much to speak of. Straw ticking for a bed, a few iron hooks mounted on the wall where a person could hang clothes to keep them off the dirty wood floor. Sarapan had stacked a few bags against a wall, as if willing to let the bottom one get fouled but not the rest. But the room had a door, which was the important thing. Sarapan closed it and looked expectantly at Conor. "Well?"

Conor drew the teeth from the pouch that dangled from his belt. He held out his closed fist, then opened it, inches from Sarapan's face. "Have you ever seen their like?"

Sarapan blinked. His mouth opened, then closed. He shook his head. "I cannot say that I have. What are they?"

"Who knows? The teeth of a god, some say," Conor bluffed. No one had said that, except he himself once it had occurred to him.

"Quite odd," Sarapan said.

"Do you like them?"

"I don't know," Sarapan replied. "I am not sure what I would do with them."

"If they are truly a god's teeth, then the market for them would be limitless," Conor said. "Not where I am headed, but back in Aquilonia."

"But how would one prove that?" Sarapan queried. "They could as easily be from some oversized hound."

"Never has there been a dog with jaws so huge," Conor protested.

"Well, some other creature then. Even a dragon or

some such. Without the rest of the head, who can say?"

"I'll let you have them for a good price," Conor pressed.

"There is no price I would pay, without knowing what they are," Sarapan said. His fat face was flushed again, this time edging toward purple.

Conor felt anger swelling in his breast. "Do you think I would cheat you?"

"I said nothing of the sort. But I am not buying those teeth, so you might as well put them away."

The futility of the whole thing suddenly struck Conor. He had not been able to sell the teeth in Aquilonia. In two days he would be in Cimmeria, then he would head west a for a few days, to Taern. No one there would care about them, or have any treasure to part with anyway. He had gone to considerable trouble, and put his own life in jeopardy, and for what? He had been sure that the Pictish crown was valuable, so therefore these parts of it were worth something, too. But if no one wanted them, then all they were was a nuisance.

He hated the way Sarapan stared at him. The miserable, pudgy merchant considered him some kind of fool, or worse. Conor had tried to give him an honest deal, a fair price. But the rage built in him as Sarapan stared, obviously trying to find a diplomatic way to get the barbarian out of his room. Now Conor couldn't tell if the man's face was even more red, or if it was just the bloodlust clouding his vision.

Without even thinking about it, he drew his broadsword from its scabbard. Sarapan's mouth worked

soundlessly, but Conor knew he was trying to give voice
to a terrified scream. He closed the distance between
them with a single step and swung the sword. Sarapan's
body crumpled to the floor, lifeless, the scream dying
inside his throat.

Conor knew he had to hurry. Someone might have
heard the altercation, recognized the sound of a body hitting the floor. The merchant had gold, he was certain.
He wouldn't have taken a private room in the inn if he
hadn't. He checked the man's body first. No luck. Turned
to the rest of the room. The bags. Digging through them,
he came across clothing—more of the same silks and
satins, for the most part. No loot.

Conor rose, surveyed the room again. If there were a
hidden panel or something, he would not find it. The
fury in him was so great that he moved to kick Sarapan's lifeless husk, but when he did, he noticed a slight
mound beneath the straw. Instead, he kicked that, re-
vealing a velvet purse.

Two dozen golden lunas spilled into his hand when
he upended it. He felt their weight for a moment, smiling. Poured them into his own purse.

Everything he owned he had on him. But he wanted
the horse from the stable. Maybe even a fresh one, if it
didn't cost more than one of his gold pieces.

After all, he had ridden his most of the day. Now he
would have to ride all night, as well. Maybe he could be
across the border before anyone found the dead man.

If not, at least he'd be well out of the reach of the local law.

And now, finally, he had a stake that would serve him well in Taern. He had accomplished what he had gone to Aquilonia for. He'd seen the civilized world, and he had gained his treasure.

Time to go home, Conor thought. *More than time.*

8

THE STREETS OF Kuthmet were much quieter now that the sun had gone. Darkness ruled the quiet hours; darkness and the Sons of Set, the serpent god. They had barely left Tarawa's house when Donial saw the first snake. It was about four feet long, black with red stripes. Torchlight gleamed off its sinuous back as it writhed its way up the road.

He noticed Tarawa glance at the thing casually, then turn her head as if it was beneath her attention. Kral, however, cringed away from the serpent. Picts hated snakes, Donial knew, and Kral was no exception. The savage's hand had dropped to his knife hilt, ready to strike at the beast. He didn't like snakes, but it was distaste, not fear, that ruled his reaction. Donial continued watching the snake until it reached a corner and slithered out of sight.

He had to step quickly to catch up with the others, who kept pace with Tarawa. Before they had gone another block, he saw two more serpents, one twice the size of the first.

Even as large as that snake was, it was not as fearsome as the one they saw on the next dark block. Tarawa gasped and pressed them all back against the nearest stone wall. "Now you see why we seldom venture out in the dark," she hissed. "Remain still—their eyesight is poor, but they can detect sudden motion."

The snake she shied from was at least thirty feet in length, Donial judged, and as big around as a barrel. Its tongue flicked from its mouth as it slithered along the road toward them, darting out to taste the air. With a slow, smooth motion, Kral slid his sword from its scabbard. Donial did the same. He didn't want to attract the thing's attention, but if they did, he wanted to be ready to defend against it. He only caught glimpses of its fangs, but they looked like daggers.

Mikelo had told them stories about the huge snakes that were allowed to roam the streets of some Stygian cities, taking any unfortunate passersby for victims. He had heard rumors of such things even back in Tarantia. But he had never quite been able to believe it. Why would anyone allow such grotesque beasts free rein?

Tarawa spoke softly, almost as if reading Donial's mind. "The priests worship Set," she explained. "The snake god. No one denies the snakes anything, for fear of enraging Set. Or at least his priests."

The thing came closer as she spoke, but it did not seem aware of their presence. It writhed past them, searching out some tastier treat. Donial breathed a sigh of relief once it had disappeared down the dark street.

"That was close," Tarawa said. "We were lucky, or blessed."

"Surely it can't eat everyone it comes into contact with," Alanya suggested. "It would not always be hungry, would it?"

"Perhaps not," Tarawa said. "But there are more than one that size."

"I find that hard to believe," Kral said.

"Be that as it may, it is true," Tarawa insisted.

"I have seen more than one during my brief time in Stygia," Mikelo said.

Kral shuddered visibly. "Once I have the Teeth, I will never again set foot in this cursed land."

"I have said much the same thing," Tarawa said, "nearly every day since I was brought here. And yet, here I am."

She was a slave, and Donial doubted that escape was an easy option for her. But he was sure that Kral would make good on his pledge. This place was as alien to the Pict as the surface of the moon, and probably less appealing.

"Have no doubts," Kral assured her. "I will not tarry here a moment longer than necessary. Now, can we get to al Nasir's place?"

Tarawa looked back toward the big snake, now completely vanished down the street. "Hurry," she urged, leading the way again. "Before we encounter another one."

A short, brisk walk later, they stood on the outskirts of an enormous compound of large, dark buildings. All were dark, hunched against the sky like crouching warriors waiting to spring. A wall surrounded the whole compound, which seemed almost as large as the entire rest of the town, but it was barely more than a man's height, as if Shehkmi al Nasir was not truly worried about intruders.

In a way, that scared Donial more than anything else.

"He is inside," Tarawa said. "If he were out, I would know of it. Anyway, for the past month or more he has almost never ventured beyond his walls. Most of his time is spent inside the temple, there in the center of the compound."

"Do we know if the Teeth has been delivered yet?" Kral asked.

Tarawa shook her head. "I think we need to go inside to find out."

"Then why do we stand here?"

"Shh!" Alanya grabbed Kral's arm. "Listen."

The group hushed immediately, and in the silence, Donial heard the sound that had alerted his sister. The unmistakable scuff of feet on the road. Many of them. Men trying to walk quietly, Donial guessed.

"Coming this way," Kral whispered. "Where can we hide?"

Tarawa pointed toward an arched gateway—one of the entrances to al Nasir's vast compound, but unguarded, it seemed. "In there!"

They hurried across the narrow street into the shadows. Here, standing so close to al Nasir's home turf, Donial felt a chill. It wasn't possible that the sorcerer could know they were here—was it? Could the people coming their way be guards sent out to fetch them?

In less than a minute he knew the truth. It was Gorian and his mercenaries, having arrived from the camp they had made the night before. They approached al Nasir's campground with all due stealth, but there were too many of them to remain completely silent. Their feet chafed the earth, their weapons and armor jingling softly with their progress.

Donial watched them approach. He didn't know what to do about their presence, if anything. Nor was there opportunity to confer with his comrades. Any word uttered now, no matter in how low a whisper, would alert their competitors to their presence. He stood, still and silent, willing them to just pass by. But then Sullas glanced their way, as if his eye had been drawn by some hidden magnet.

"There!" he said, glaring into the shadowed archway. Pointing.

He stood there still when the snake shot from an alley and caught him in its enormous mouth.

KRAL DREW HIS sword from its scabbard for the second time since they had left Tarawa's house. This time, he fully expected to use it—but on men, not on some horrific beast. That was before the creature exploded into the midst of the mercenaries, though. Its gaping maw clamped across Sullas's middle, splitting the man virtually in two. With a single, horrible bite, it swallowed Sullas's lower half. The hardened mercenaries screamed with panic. Among them, the snake—even bigger than the last one they'd seen—writhed and bucked, fangs flashing in moonlight as it lunged at another of the soldiers.

Other soldiers tried to fight the thing, their blades hacking and slashing at it. But the snake whipped its massive tail and smashed six of them against the compound's wall. The cuts of the others didn't seem to slow the thing at all.

Kral felt Mikelo's hand on his arm, holding him back. "If it kills them, so much the better," the boy said.

"If it kills them, we're next," Kral countered. He pulled free of Mikelo's hand and charged into the fray.

The snake exuded a foul, fetid odor, as if it had only just crawled out from the depths of hell itself. Its skin was pebbled, gray-black. It moved with a grace that Kral found at once repulsive and strangely beautiful. That didn't keep him from slashing at it with the keen edge of his blade. But the snake ignored the blow. It crushed a soldier underneath it, then turned its attention to the newcomer.

Kral was almost hypnotized by the eyes locked on his. They were golden in color, penetrating, with pupils like dark, bottomless slits. They stared unblinkingly at him, and he thought he could easily fall into them and never come out. A strange, awful intelligence seemed to inhabit those eyes, as if the creature might begin speaking in its own odd and sibilant tongue, sharing all the knowledge its kind had amassed over the eons. Perhaps this was why some worshiped snakes, why they let them roam the streets freely.

Kral shut his eyes tightly and struck out with the sword just before the snake lunged at him, its fangs dripping liquid poison. When he dared look, the tip of his sword had become embedded in the snake's forehead, just above the right eye. Thick green blood welled up around the wound. When Kral yanked his blade free, it jetted toward him as if from a fountain, splashing him with a hot, acidic stream.

The snake jerked away from him, writhing in pain. As it did, its coils wrapped around some of the mercenaries, who hacked and stabbed at it with their own weapons. Even wounded, the thing was supremely powerful, and one of the men dropped his sword as his shoulders and head turned red, then purple. Others started trying to slash their way to him, to free him, but before they could do so, he slumped over onto the snake's back, dead.

After wiping off as much of the snake's burning blood as he could, Kral turned his full attentions back to it. He approached its head again, dodging its snapping jaws. The head lunged toward Kral, and he swatted it with the flat of his blade. It retreated, then came again from a different angle. This time, Kral stabbed upward when the head neared him. His sword cut up through the beast's chin, shattering teeth. As it tried to back away,

Kral held the sword still, and the snake ripped a huge gash in its own lower jaw.

It let out a kind of keening wail, a sound unlike any Kral had ever dreamed snakes could make. Its acidic blood splashed everywhere. Its writhing sped up, as if in a panic, and Kral heard several of the men cry out in pain.

Finally, the snake slumped to the ground as if all its muscles relaxed in sequence, tail to head. The head twitched a couple more times, the horrible golden eyes staring at him with their own weird intelligence, even in death.

Kral shuddered, glad the confrontation was over. His flesh burned where the blood had spattered him, and his ribs ached where the stab wound he'd gotten from the pirate captain Kunios had been aggravated by the struggle. He bent at the waist, hands on his knees, to catch his breath. As he did, Alanya, Donial, and Mikelo came over to him.

"Good job, Kral!" Donial enthused. "Had it not been for your efforts that monster would likely have defeated all of those mercenaries."

Kral nodded wearily, and when he raised his head, Gorian stood before him.

"The boy is correct," Gorian said. "We owe you a debt of gratitude."

"I did it for us, not for you," Kral said. "The lot of you would likely not have sated the appetite of so great a creature."

Gorian smiled. "Nonetheless, you and my men battled together, side by side. Since I can only assume that our objectives here in Kuthmet are similar—else why lurk outside the compound of the sorcerer Shehkmi al Nasir?—perhaps we should consider continuing the partnership begun here."

"I doubt that our objectives are the same," Kral answered. "I seek to save the Pictish people from certain destruction. Is your cause as clear or worthwhile?"

Gorian hesitated for only a moment. "I know nothing of a threat to the Picts, or any other people," he admitted. "I know only that I seek, on behalf of one I serve, a Pictish crown that has come into the possession of the Stygian."

"Then our immediate goal is the same," Kral said. "I also seek the crown. But it is after the gaining of it that our intentions surely differ."

"True enough," Gorian said. His arms were crossed casually over his chest. "Why not ally our efforts, until such time as we have seized it? Mitra knows we'll have a fight on our hands with al Nasir."

"And when we have it, what then?" Donial asked. "We fight each other?"

"Depending on who is left alive at that time, the issue may have settled itself," Gorian said. "Or perhaps there's a way we can both achieve our ends. Whatever you plan to do with the crown may not conflict with what my master desires. It just seems foolish not to combine our forces in order to give ourselves the best chance against the sorcerer."

"I agree," Alanya put in. "We know not what we face inside, and even Tarawa can only provide so much assistance. The lot of us working together have a better chance at success than just a few. And if we're competing with one another for it, our chances are lessened even more."

Kral found himself swayed by these arguments. If both groups tried, independently of the other, to get the crown, they would only get in each other's way. Chances were Shehkmi al Nasir would be able to play them against each other and retain the Teeth for himself. Working together would increase their chances.

And he had no doubt that, when they had the crown, he would be able to defeat Gorian in combat. The number of mercenaries at his disposal had been severely depleted by one fight after another, and some had not survived the battle with the snake. He counted but six remaining, Gorian included. Most were wounded, a couple bleeding seriously, though they bound their wounds with strips of fabric cut from their clothing.

Team up now, fight whoever was left for possession of the Teeth. That was a plan Kral could live with.

9

INSIDE THE COMPOUND of Shehkmi al Nasir, three acolytes walked torchlit passageways, their slippered feet almost silent on the worn stone floors. Two led the way, one carrying a censer that filled their way with strong incense and the other a small chime that gave soft musical tones with every step. Behind them, the third held an ornately carved wooden box, inlaid with precious gems and tiled designs of indescribable beauty. Inside the box, nestled in a bed of black velvet, was the Pictish crown they had acquired in Tarantia. The three chanted quietly, repeating a tune whose words had long since lost their meaning to all but the most dedicated scholars of ancient days.

The acolyte who carried the box allowed himself a quick smile. He knew this was a solemn occasion and that his master was not a man who appreciated humor or moments of self-congratulation. But the acolyte was young. He had only been in the service of al Nasir for a little more than two years. In that time, he had worked hard to gain his master's favor. Al Nasir demonstrated that favor in only small ways, but each time he did the acolyte felt an inner thrill that he had pleased the powerful sorcerer. Having achieved this, having brought the crown that al Nasir claimed would help increase his power, could not fail to raise his status in the master's eyes.

Al Nasir had not said precisely that he would—or could—challenge Thoth Amon for position as the most powerful servant of Set in the land. Nonetheless, the acolyte thought that might be the case. There could only be two outcomes, he knew, to such a challenge. The likeliest was that Thoth Amon would smite Shehkmi al Nasir with every weapon at his disposal and render the whole compound smoking rubble. In that case, the acolyte would die in his master's service, which would ensure him safe passage down the River Styx to the land of the dead. But the other possibility was that al Nasir would win the struggle. In that case, he would doubtless bestow great favor and blessings on the ones who had brought him the crown that had made his victory possible.

So the acolyte allowed himself a momentary sense of accomplishment, and thought about the rewards that would follow, in this world or the next. He and his partners had been assigned a difficult task, and they had

prevailed. Soon he would deliver the inlaid box into his
master's waiting hands, and his world would change
forever.

TARAWA LED THE way into al Nasir's huge complex
of buildings. Within, silence reigned; silence and darkness seemed to fill the space inside the walls like liquid would fill a barrel. Alanya could tell that structures
hulked around them, because their black shapes blotted
out the stars from the sky. But she could get no sense
of detail from the buildings themselves—they might
have been adobe and wood, like Tarawa's house, or they
might have been gilded palaces.

With each one they passed, Alanya's sensation of
dread grew. Surely someone must be inside these quiet
buildings. Watching their progress. Measuring the threat
they posed, if any. Waiting for the right moment to un-
leash horrible Stygian magics at them.

But Tarawa paid the structures no mind. She had a
destination, and she led the group directly there without
hesitation. They came to a narrow doorway. Tarawa
threw back the bolt with practiced familiarity. "This is a
slaves' entrance," she whispered as she did so. "No one
else uses it, and few even know of its existence. Often
Shehkmi likes to have one or more of us visit privately,
without taking the chance of running into his acolytes
or other household servants."

"Where will it take us?" Kral asked.

"Directly to the innermost chambers of his temple,"

Tarawa answered. Inside the doorway, a torch flickered in a sconce on the wall. She reached up and took it down. "Which is where he is most likely to receive the delivery of the object you seek."

"Is there any way to intercept those bringing it?" he asked. "If we are not too late for that."

"Perhaps," Tarawa replied. "These corridors pass by the more commonly used ones, and there are secret panels of which none but we slaves, and Shehkmi himself, know. I have heard that the sorcerer who built it, long before Shehkmi al Nasir's time, had the architects and builders put to death once the compound was finished, though I know not if those stories are true."

Once they had passed inside, Tarawa led with her torch held high, through a corridor barely more than three feet wide. The floor was noticeably slanted, and Alanya could tell they descended rapidly beneath the surface. Conversation ceased. The eleven of them moved as quietly as they could, although the mercenaries' mail shirts jangled as they walked, and their boots scuffed on the smooth stone floor. Alanya feared someone would hear them in spite of their attempts at stealth. The more time she spent in the Stygian sorcerer's compound, the more she came to believe that this whole quest was a horrifically bad idea.

Her fear was confirmed a few minutes later.

The group neared an intersection illuminated by a quartet of torches set into wall sconces at the corners. Tarawa had explained, in a low whisper, that these torches were mystically fueled and never went out, bringing constant light to otherwise pitch-black passageways. Above

the sconces were carved snake heads, staring out into the
intersection from every corner.

The walls, Alanya noted as they went, were unadorned
but worn smooth, as the floor was, by the passage of time
and many people. About hand high there was an indenta-
tion, as if people over the eons had walked by, rubbing
their hands along that one spot.

As they entered the intersection, Alanya saw that here,
the walls were decorated with hundreds of drawings,
overlaying each other as if they had been applied over
the centuries. A common theme was snakes, of course,
but there were other things depicted as well—including,
much to Alanya's dismay, a scene showing rank after
rank of headless women, presumably sacrificed to Set
for some unclean purpose.

She shivered. A hand on her shoulder startled her,
but she managed not to scream. Gorian stood behind
her, and she realized she had halted in her tracks, block-
ing the way of the others. With a false smile, Gorian and
a couple of his men pushed past her and deeper into the
intersection.

"You could look at these for hours," Tarawa whispered, standing close beside Alanya. "But I believe we
are in a greater hurry than that."

"I know," Alanya said. She started to turn away from
the weird images. As she did, she heard a strange puffing
noise from farther ahead, in the center of the intersection.

She looked past Tarawa and saw blurs dart out from the
mouth of one of the snake sculptures, which had seemingly come to life and spat something. Gorian slapped a

hand to his neck, surprised, as if he'd been stung by an insect. But in less than a second, his expression changed, his mouth falling slack, eyes rolling up into his head. Then his knees gave out, and he plunged to the floor. When he hit, his hand fell away from his neck and a hole was revealed there. It looked to Alanya like an arrow hole, of which she had seen a few back in Koronaka. But no arrow jutted from it, just a thin line of blood flowing onto the floor. The small stone that always hung on a leather thong around his neck had fallen out of his shirt and landed in the stream of blood. Kral had speculated that the stone was the source of Gorian's magic, but it had done nothing to save him this time.

The worst of it was not over, however. As she watched, a tiny snake's head, no bigger around than her smallest finger, poked out from the wound. It wriggled out of the hole, then writhed quickly away down the cross corridor, disappearing into the darkness. On the wall, the stone snake shifted almost imperceptibly, once more taking on the appearance of nothing but a simple sculpture. She wondered if her eyes were playing tricks.

"Mitra!" the mercenary named Dalthus exclaimed. Another let out a loud gasp of horror.

"Quiet!" Kral reminded them. "We know not who might be about!"

The mercenaries looked upon their fallen leader with terror—which Alanya shared. In the uneven light, Mikelo looked pale and terrified. Donial had a look of strange fascination on his face. Only Kral seemed relatively unaffected by what they had seen.

"A trap," he said. "Meant to strike down the first into the intersection."

"But we slaves use this passageway all the time," Tarawa protested. "And it has never attacked us."

"You are meant to be here. Somehow, al Nasir's trap can distinguish those who should be here from intruders." So saying, Kral stepped into the center of the intersection, across Gorian's corpse. Alanya could tell that he was keeping a close eye on the remaining snake sculptures, but they were still.

A couple of the mercenaries watched every step he took with increasing terror. "A simple trap I can understand," Galados said, his voice trembling. "But that . . . that snake—it was not a snake when it hit Gorian."

"Some kind of dart," another agreed. His voice was too loud, Alanya thought, his fear trumping caution. "This is sorcery of the worst kind."

"We're in the compound of a fearsome Stygian mage," Donial pointed out. "What do you expect?"

"It is exactly what I do expect that I fear," Galados said. His eyes were wide with horror, and spittle flecked the corners of his mouth. "I fully expect more magical attacks. But now the man who was supposed to pay us is dead."

"He hired you on behalf of another," Kral reminded them. "Or so he said."

"He did," the one named Shulev admitted. "And we could take the crown back to Tarantia, and probably get paid for our troubles. Probably. But Gorian was the one we knew—I know not if we could even find the one he served when we got there."

"If you got there," Kral said. "As I have every intention of taking the crown home with me."

Alanya was shocked that Kral would remind the mercenaries of that, at this moment. She fully expected them to charge him with swords drawn, determined to settle the issue before another moment passed.

But they didn't. Kral had read them better than she did, apparently. Instead of attacking, they looked almost subdued, beaten before they even tried. "If I knew there would be gold at the end of it, Pict, we would find out right now who the better man is," the first one said. The others seemed to look to this one for guidance, now that Sullas and Gorian were gone. A couple looked close to blubbering. They were hardened fighting men, but she supposed that Stygian sorcery was a different sort of foe than they had faced before—one not easily bested with mere steel. "But there are no guarantees, and our chances are looking worse, not better. If I walk away with my life, I'll have more opportunities to seek treasure elsewhere."

"Aye," Hakon grumbled. "Right you are. Anyway, who knows what trap may be sprung on us next? If the very walls are against us, there's no winning."

"I'm with you," Shelko said, jutting his chin toward Gorian's corpse. "I've no interest in meeting my end like that. Let's take our leave while we can still walk."

Tarawa shushed them. Alanya didn't miss the fear in

the slave girl's voice as she did. She, of them all, knew best what dangers might await them here under the earth.

There was more subdued mumbling from the men, but they had reached their conclusion. Even as they turned and headed back the way they had come, they seemed to relax, as if emboldened by their decision to give in to their horror. Alanya watched them go with mixed feelings. It would make things easier when they got the crown, if they didn't have to battle their own allies. But if getting the crown involved a fight, they might need all the swords they could get.

"Let them go," Kral said, disgust tinging his voice. "Cowards like those will be no help to us."

"But they could still alert the Stygian somehow," Mikelo pointed out.

"Why would they?" Donial asked. "What would they gain by it? More likely they would sacrifice their lives."

"Donial's right," Kral said. "Come, let's continue on our way and never think of those dogs again."

As the men disappeared up the dark slope, Alanya couldn't help wishing that it was the other way around— she and her friends giving up, and those battle-tested soldiers descending farther into al Nasir's den.

But she was here with Kral, and he was not the kind to retreat. Instead, he started down the ramp, and Tarawa had to hurry to pass him so she could lead the way.

10

USAM SAT ON a downed log in the depths of the forest, catching his breath. Through the trees he could see the glow of the flames that scorched the high walls of Koronaka. He had been at the wall a short while before, in the thick of the action. He had been there when one of the big gates had opened and soldiers had charged the Pictish force. He was glad they had tried it—shooting arrows into the fort only provided minimal pleasure. Usam liked to see his enemies die. When possible, he liked to separate their heads from their bodies. He had not enjoyed enough of that so far, but when the settlers came headlong into the Pictish ranks, he found plenty of amusement.

But he knew he was also needed away from the fort, guiding the others, providing direction and inspiration.

As he had planned, the unified Pictish force had agreed to operate under his command, and he couldn't plan strategy and strike off the heads of the settlers at the same time. He was accustomed to leading a clan's worth of warriors, not an army numbering in the thousands. It made his head hurt to think of all the things that had to be considered, so he sat on the tree trunk away from the battle and tried to scheme.

The main force had surrounded the fort, coming out of the trees just after sunset with volley after volley of arrows. After softening up the defenses that way, they had added some flaming arrows into the mix. The settlers had tried to respond with arrows of their own, but the Picts had an entire forest to shield them, and the trees took more shafts than their warriors did. Which left the settlers no way to respond, once their walls started to burn, but to engage the Picts on their own ground.

Which was the next thing to suicide. In the trees, with vastly superior numbers, the Picts were unbeatable. They were painted to blend in with the night, they were fierce and determined, and once battle was joined the bloodlust took them over.

The settlers had since realized their mistake. A handful of Picts got in through the gate before it was closed again, and those Aquilonians unfortunate enough to be outside the wall were sacrificed. As, Usam was sure, were the Picts who made it into the fort. The question before him was, now what? Wait until the walls burned to cinders, then attack? But what if the settlers got the fires extinguished? Then the whole raid might have been for naught. They'd have taken some lives, but that in itself was not good enough. They needed to get inside the walls, to find the Teeth of the Ice Bear, if the sacred relic was still within.

While he pondered the question, Usam heard a crash in the underbrush. Someone headed his way. And not a Pict, else he would have heard nothing. He had a spear with him, and a war axe. But the spear was lying across his lap, so he got to his feet, raised his spear. A few seconds later, by the uneven glow of the distant flames, he saw a soldier from the fort. The man wore a helmet, carried a shield, and underneath his leather cuirass was a mail shirt. No wonder he made so much noise in the woods, Usam thought. In the soldier's eyes he saw a look of disorientation, almost panic. The man had probably come out in the wave of soldiers, avoided instant massacre, and become lost in the dense trees.

Usam waited another moment while the soldier looked about helplessly. Then he charged, spear out, war cry tearing from his lips. The soldier reacted instantly, lifting his shield and using it to deflect Usam's initial thrust. At the same time, he uttered a surprised grunt and swung his short sword. It whistled harmlessly past Usam. The Pictish chief jabbed with the spear again, but the soldier brought his sword back around in time to block it. Almost as if in a frenzy, he started flailing toward Usam with the sword. Usam blocked the blows with his spear. The blade bit chunks from the shaft of Usam's weapon, and the Pict found himself driven back, back by the man's unceasing advance.

Branches scraped against Usam's back, tangled in his long hair. It was not possible that this Aquilonian could beat him, not in the forest. But his weapon was being whittled down to nothing and he could not manage to gut the civilized pig. He stabbed with the spear fruitlessly, then brought the shaft up to block another overhand swing, and the soldier's sword cleaved right through what was left of the spear.

Usam hurled the pieces at the soldier's head and raced into the forest. He clutched at his knife as he ran, drawing it from its scabbard. He did not want to fight the soldier with only that, although he would if necessary. But he'd left his war axe back beside the fallen tree. That was what he sought now. His mistake had been leaving it behind in the first place. This persistent Aquilonian was just begging to have his head lopped off. The battle had taken him away from the tree, but he was a Pict, and in the forest he could not get lost.

A minute later, less maybe, and he was there. The axe waited where he had left it. The soldier was right behind, crashing through the trees like a deranged bear. Usam didn't even slow his pace, just hurdled the log and snatched up his axe with one hand. Once he had his grip, he stopped, whirled around, swinging it neck high. The soldier had just blundered into the little clearing. All his momentum was propelling him forward, and when he saw the axe he couldn't stop.

The axe bit through his neck. His head sailed across the clearing, bouncing off a tree at its edge. Usam, panting, smiled as he watched the twitching body tumble, blood from its open neck staining the fallen leaves.

He should have taken the axe in the first place. Should have waited another few seconds, until he determined the nature of the threat, before rushing into action. He realized the same could apply to the greater question of Koronaka. They needed to get the Teeth back to the guardian's cave, but that did not necessarily have to happen tonight. The Teeth had been gone for weeks, now. Longer. Sooner would be better than later, but if the fort did not fall tonight, then it would the night after, or the one after that.

There was urgency, but not panic. Not yet. None knew how long they had before the Ice Bear returned. But it had been so long already—chances were, a few more days would not hurt. Meanwhile, the settlers were imprisoned within their own walls. They had no way out, and unless reinforcements came from Aquilonia, the Picts would soon overwhelm them.

DALTHUS LED THE way back out of the temple. It was impossible for them to get lost, as the crossing where Gorian had breathed his last was the only one they had encountered thus far. Even so, without a torch he was anxious. The darkness seemed to squeeze his throat like the murderous hands of a strangler. He struggled to find his breath.

Behind him, one of the men cleared his throat, then did so again. "Silence," Dalthus urged. "We are not in the clear yet."

But the man kept at it, making hoarse, ragged sounds. Finally, Dalthus stopped in his tracks, turned around. It was almost pitch-black, and he couldn't see the men at all, could only make out the faintest impression of their silhouettes. He could locate the one making all the racket, however, by the sound. He pushed past a couple of the others and reached for where the man's shoulder should have been. But the man—he was certain by now that it was Shelko, the oldest of the surviving mercenaries, pitched forward as Dalthus was reaching, and fell into him. Dalthus wrapped his arms around his fellow to hold him upright. As he did, he felt a writhing movement near the man's neck. With a repulsed shriek he shoved Shelko away, slamming the man into a wall. A hissing sound confirmed his fear— a snake had somehow wrapped itself around Shelko's neck, and now that the man was unconscious, or worse, it tried to strike out toward another victim.

Dalthus batted it away with the back of his arm. "Snake!" he warned the others.

"Where?" one shouted.

"Shelko!" Dalthus started to reply. But as he opened his mouth to do so, something filled it with a rush.

The snake, he knew. Or another one. Even as the horrible realization set in, he could feel the thing twitching about in his open mouth, fangs snapping at the lining of his cheeks. He tried to yank the creature away, or to bite down on it and kill it that way. But he was unable to accomplish either.

In seconds, the inside of his mouth felt as if it were

on fire. He tried to scream, but with the snake there could only get out a muffled groan. He felt the strength ebbing from his muscles. If it hadn't already been dark, he suspected it would have become so.

Just before he died, he heard the other men with him screaming in pain and fear. Snakes, one of them said.

Here, it was always snakes.

KRAL DIDN'T WANT to admit it to the others, but he felt an increasing sense of dread as they went lower and lower into the temple. The place was thick with dark magics, and he didn't like it at all.

He kept his concerns to himself. He didn't mind so much that the mercenaries had left, but he didn't want to alarm his friends any more than necessary. They would have trouble enough on their hands once they found the Teeth.

Tarawa seemed oddly casual about leading them to her master's secret lair. Kral wasn't sure how to interpret that. Was she drawing them into a trap? Or did she really just hate al Nasir so much that she would take advantage of any opportunity to cause him displeasure? He hoped it was the latter.

But he kept his hand on the hilt of his knife and Tarawa's back in front of him, just in case . . .

11

IN THIS CHAMBER, Shehkmi al Nasir allowed himself physical comfort. A fireplace warded off winter's chill. In the rare event that it grew warm, so far below the surface, there were fans that could be operated by slaves tugging on cords. There were soft, padded couches on which he could nap or, if he preferred, be entertained by one of his more attractive servants. He kept casks of fine wine down here. It was his retreat from the demands the rest of his life placed on him—the constant quest for more and deeper wisdom, the struggle to increase his power and influence throughout the shadowy reaches of the hierarchy of Set.

So he waited, lounging in a pillowed corner with a cloud of incense overhanging the room, for the delivery of the Pictish crown. The power inherent in that artifact would, he believed, give him the means to overturn the balance that existed.

Presently he heard the rasp of slippered feet in the corridor. His acolytes, bringing him the prize, which he had wrested right out from under the nose of his Aquilonian "friend" Kanilla Rey. Suppressing a smile, he sat up straight until they entered the chamber, then rose to meet them.

"Do you have it?" he asked. He already knew the answer. But tradition dictated certain rules be followed.

"We have it," the three acolytes intoned together. They wore matching hooded robes. Their heads were all shorn under their hoods. They had dark eyes and dusky skin. They might have been three slightly different versions of the same man. Which was the point—by eliminating individual characteristics, they were able to focus on their servitude to Set.

And, of course, to Shehkmi al Nasir.

He held both hands out toward a small wooden table. The two acolytes in front stepped to the sides, allowing the one behind, carrying an inlaid box, to come forward. He put the box down on the table and removed the lid.

The crown inside was even less impressive than al Nasir had expected.

It was undeniably ancient. A collection of small bones, most of which looked human but might also have included the bones of a bear's paw. Some of them had been joined with strips of flesh originally, but at some point in the past bits of copper wire had reinforced it. Set into the circle of bones, jutting up from the crown, were enormous teeth that looked like a bear's. Surely no bear that size had ever walked the Earth, at least not within the memory of man.

The ugly thing might have sat in some shop for decades, gathering dust. But the sorcerer knew that it had not.

When he picked it up from the box, he knew why.

His hands tingled, then his arms. Finally, his entire body felt charged, energized. The little crown radiated power. Now he allowed himself a smile. He had made the right decision, taking this powerful object away from Kanilla Rey and having it brought here. The Aquilonian wasn't a good enough magician to know how to use the crown properly, and al Nasir was certain that even if he could have figured it out, his goals would have been petty.

He held the crown for a few moments, then put it back into the box. It was only then, looking down on it, that he noticed what was wrong.

"It's missing teeth!" he shouted angrily. "Where are they?"

The acolytes were too frightened to answer in unison. The one who had borne the box said, "This is as we found it."

"I sent you for the *whole* crown," Shehkmi al Nasir raged. "Not *part* of it. Yes, it is a powerful artifact. But like this . . . its power is minimized, reduced. It is not whole. It is not what I commanded you to bring me."

"We . . . we had no way to know," the acolyte protested. "We had never seen it before, knew only that we were to bring you the crown that we discovered where you told us to look."

Al Nasir knew the man spoke truth. But as powerful as the thing was now, whole it would have been far more so. He had not counted on pieces of it having been removed, leaving obvious, gaping holes where they had rested for eons unknown.

Fury built inside him, and it needed release. He performed a quick spell, so familiar to him that he had only to think it. In his right hand, a tiny ball of energy grew to the size of a fist. He held his hand up toward the acolyte who had spoken, and uttered a single word. The acolyte's face registered shock as his chest bulged, then fabric and flesh rent themselves. His heart burst from its enclosure and flew to al Nasir's outstretched hand, where it was quickly consumed by the pulsating energy there. When al Nasir closed his hand, heart and energy ball had both vanished.

"Such is the price of failure," he said. The two remaining acolytes looked at the floor, rather than at the fallen corpse of their comrade or at their master. "Now go. Leave me. I would find those missing teeth, and I need privacy for that task."

The acolytes backed out of the chamber as fast as they could, and within moments al Nasir could hear them hurtling headlong up the corridor away from him. They would have second thoughts about their service, perhaps. But if they stayed on, they would be careful never to fail their master again.

"MISSING TEETH?" KRAL whispered. They stood behind a screened-off door through which they could just barely see what was happening in the chamber beyond. Alanya had been afraid that he could see them, but Tarawa had assured them that the screen was positioned in such a way as to keep the door invisible to anyone in the room, since al Nasir didn't want his acolytes or other visitors to know about the special entrance.

"Silence," Tarawa replied, raising a warning hand. "Just wait . . ."

Moments later, Alanya saw what they were waiting for. With a last, furious glance at the crown, Shehkmi al Nasir stormed out of the chamber through an intricately carved door. The body of the slain acolyte lay where it had fallen.

"He never performs magic in that room," Tarawa explained.

"Then how did he kill that man?" Mikelo wondered.

"Almost never. Not serious magic," she elucidated. "Killing someone like that, for him, is as easy as breathing or swallowing for you and me. But to find what happened to any missing teeth from that crown will require a more intense effort. He has a special room for that, with all of his magical equipment and tools in it. This is more a place for reflection or relaxation."

"But . . . he left the crown sitting there!" Kral pointed out.

"He must not need it for the spell he plans," Tarawa reasoned.

"Does anything prevent us from going in and taking it now?"

"If it doesn't matter that it is not complete," she answered.

"It does," Kral said. "We need the whole thing, ultimately. But I doubt the missing teeth are here in Stygia. Better to take what we can now and find the rest ourselves."

Frustration caused Alanya to clench her fists so hard that her fingernails dug into her palms. To have come so close to the prize they sought, and now this!

She tried to remember in whose hands the crown had been. It must have been whole in its cavern beneath the Bear Clan's village, she reasoned. Then Uncle Lupinius had stolen it. He had carried it with him to Tarantia, where he'd taken refuge in the home of her late father. A thief had stolen the crown from him, then the Stygians, according to Conor, had taken it from the thief. If they didn't have all the teeth, then it must have been the thief who took them.

Him, or . . .

"Conor!"

"The Cimmerian you hired?" Kral asked. "What about him?"

"We should have known better than to trust that lout," she said. "He might have taken them from the thief who stole the crown from our uncle. At the very least, he would have been among those who had access to them, and he never mentioned them to us."

"You could be right," Kral said. "That thief had the crown for long enough to have removed some. If Conor took them . . . Is he still in Tarantia?"

"He disappeared before we left," Donial said. "No doubt headed home to Cimmeria. That's what he said he was planning. He never did care for civilized life."

"That's the one thing we share, then," Kral said. "But we tarry too long. Tarawa, open the door."

She did so. Kral passed through, nervously entering the wizard's chamber. Nothing stopped him, however, and within seconds he was back at the door with the crown's container in his hands. "We'll transfer it to something less showy after we get out of here," he said. "Now, Tarawa, how fast can we leave this place?"

Alanya had never heard more beautiful words in her life. Leaving the sorcerer's den seemed like the best idea a human mind had ever conceived. Tarawa hoisted her torch high and led the way back up the same tunnels that had brought them here, but faster, with less regard for stealth. Kral followed, carrying the crown in its container, then Alanya and Mikelo, with Donial in the rear. With every step toward the surface, Alanya felt her spirits rising.

Coming across Gorian's body brought her a momentary panic, but they made it through that intersection with no trouble. Farther along, Tarawa's torch illuminated the bodies of the other mercenaries. None of them had made it out, it seemed.

"If they could not gain the exit, how will we?" Mikelo asked anxiously. "They had not even stolen anything from al Nasir."

Tarawa hesitated to answer, and her uncertainty sent fear through Alanya like a bolt of lightning. "I know not," she admitted. "Unless it is as Kral suggested, that because I am known here, the traps that lie in wait for others allow us passage."

"I should not like to rely on that," Kral said. "But I see little choice."

"Let's not tarry then," Donial urged. "Before whatever force controls them changes its mind."

Tarawa seemed to agree with him. She swallowed hard and stepped around the bodies scattered on the passageway floor with eyes wide, hands hooked into claws, as if they had tried to catch whatever had slain them.

Whether she was right or not, Alanya would never know. But nothing attacked them as they made their way up the narrow corridor. In less time than she would have believed possible they were back out into the cool night air of the desert. There were undoubtedly dangers yet to be encountered—the great snakes, for example, were certainly still on the hunt. But soon enough, the walls of al Nasir's compound were in sight, and Alanya felt that she could finally breathe again.

When they could see the gate through which they

had entered, Mikelo broke into a sprint. Alanya tried to catch him, but missed, and dared not call out to him. Nothing interrupted his dash, though. Almost before the others could react, he had his hands on the gate's bolt and was drawing it open. But as she watched—and it could have been a trick of the faint moonlight painting the scene with its silvery glow, but she didn't think so—the bolt wriggled in his hands, lunged, and bit Mikelo's hand.

It had only been a snake for a second, maybe less. By the time the boy crumpled to the dirt, it was nothing more than a bolt again. They ran across the empty space to him, but he was dead when they reached him. Like the mercenaries inside, he had died with his eyes wide open, as if staring at something he would never see.

Tears sprang to Alanya's eyes. "Mikelo . . ." she said. "He should never have—"

"He died free," Donial interrupted. "To him, that was the most important thing. Not to be a prisoner of those Argossean pirates anymore—that was all that mattered."

"True enough," Kral said. "You knew him best, of us, Donial. But that is what I believe, as well."

Alanya dabbed at her cheek. "I suppose you're right," she admitted. She was going to say more, but Tarawa had the gate open.

"Come," she said. "We have spent enough time here and lost enough lives. When Shehkmi discovers his prize missing, he'll be furious. I would rather not be close by when he does."

None could argue with her reasoning. Even the great snakes beyond the compound's walls held less fear for them than Shehkmi al Nasir's wrath. The relief Alanya felt at putting the place completely behind her overwhelmed even her sorrow at Mikelo's loss.

Still, as they returned to Tarawa's house through Kuthmet's night-shrouded lanes, she could not erase from her mind the image of that bolt turning into a quick-striking snake, and back again, as fast as the eye could follow.

And as she saw that, she wondered what kind of trouble they had taken on when they had decided to steal from Shehkmi al Nasir.

12

BACK IN TARAWA'S small house, Kral opened the box and took out the Teeth of the Ice Bear. The crown was not beautiful in itself, but he was surprisingly moved by the experience of holding it. It was a part of his history, his heritage as a son of the Bear Clan. He had never held the crown, had only seen it a couple of times, during rituals held in the Guardian's cave. But there was no mistaking it.

"We need to replace that fancy box," he said. "Carrying that around would attract all manner of attention to it. Have you a sack or something, Tarawa?"

"I can probably find one," she said.

"Good. Then we must figure out where to go and how to get there."

"Cimmeria," Donial reminded him. "We believe that's where Conor would have gone. I know he mentioned the name of his village."

Alanya had screwed up her face. "Taern!" she burst out. "I have been trying to remember it ever since we found out the teeth were missing. If Conor had not boasted so about his status there, I would never have remembered."

"Cimmeria is far from here," Tarawa pointed out. "How will you travel?"

"The *Restless Heart*!" Donial said.

"But the sailors are still on it," Alanya protested. "And Elonius, last of the mercenaries, with them."

"Then they'll accept me as their captain," Kral said. "Or they'll die trying to keep us off."

"But are we enough to sail her?" Alanya asked. "And if we fight them and win, what then? The three of us could never do it."

"Four," Tarawa corrected.

"You would leave Stygia and accompany us?"

"She is no longer safe here," Kral said.

"Kral speaks the truth," Tarawa agreed. "Shehkmi will figure out who let you in. His magic will reveal it to him. I have as much reason as you to want to be away from here as soon as possible."

Alanya nodded. Kral suspected that she was worried about what would happen when they returned to the ship without Gorian and the others. She was right in guessing that the *Heart*'s sailors would not readily accept them.

But there was every likelihood that they were anxious to be away from Stygian waters, no matter who was aboard.

"And I believe I can find a few more who would love to put Stygia behind," Tarawa added. "So we should be able to form a crew for your ship."

"Not our ship," Kral amended. "At least, not yet. But it will be."

GOVERNOR SHARZEN LISTENED to the continuing chaos outside with a growing sense of dread. For a second night, the walls had held against the Pictish assault. But how much longer could they last? Fires burned throughout the fort. Waves of attacks came and went, as Picts climbed the walls or broke through the burned-out sections. Runners had come back from the farther reaches of the wall with reports that Picts had overwhelmed it, simply circling around where it had not yet connected to the next fort up the line.

From all appearances, the Pictish clans had banded together. Sharzen didn't know if their goal was the complete elimination of all settlements from the Westermarck, or just of Koronaka. But Koronaka alone could not stand against them indefinitely, certainly not without reinforcements from Aquilonia. A couple of scouts had arrived claiming that reinforcements had, in fact, been sent.

At this point, it appeared that they would be too late to help.

Sharzen had no intention of dying here on the frontier.

To help figure a way out of this, he had summoned Gestian. The captain stood before him now, pacing, anxious. "You would rather be out there," Sharzen observed. "On the wall."

"I belong where my men are fighting," Gestian answered.

"Which is precisely why I made you captain of my forces," Sharzen said. "I admire that."

"Yet you have called for me," Gestian pointed out.

"Indeed," Sharzen said. "Koronaka is doomed, Gestian."

"How can you say that, Governor?"

"I say it because it is true," Sharzen replied. "Perhaps not on this night. But the next, or the one after that. Our losses these last two nights have been serious, would you not agree?"

"I would," Gestian said. "Serious, if not cataclysmic."

"So if they return tomorrow night—which they will—they will finish us?"

"Likely they will," Gestian admitted.

"When they breach the walls, think you that they will leave any survivors at all?"

Gestian paused before answering. He was covered in blood and soot from the night's battles, and his eyes glowered as if from behind a black-and-red-streaked mask. "We left none in the Bear Clan village," he noted, crossing to a window and looking out. Sharzen could see the uneven light from the flames flicker across the captain's face and armor. "It seems safest to assume that they will leave none here."

"This is my feeling as well," Sharzen acknowledged. "Our chances of surviving this are slim. The reinforcements Conan has sent are still days away. I would prefer not to breathe my last away from Aquilonian soil."

"Do you have an idea?" Gestian asked. "A plan of some kind?"

"More of a notion," Sharzen said. "I suspect that as yesterday, when the sun rises, the Picts will pull back. They know that darkness is their friend, darkness and the forest hide them from us. I propose that we take advantage of that fact. As soon as the sun rises, those of us left alive abandon Koronaka and make for Tanasul."

"Do you really think we'll reach it?"

"Not without a fight," Sharzen replied. He let his eyes drift over his office—the physical symbol of his authority here, and the height of his career. He doubted that he would have much of a career after this. There might be a way to salvage it, but he would have to wait and see once he reached Aquilonia. If not, he would, at the very least, take with him as many valuables as he could manage. "There are certainly Picts watching the fort during daylight hours. They will see us, raise the alarm, give chase. But at least we will be on the move, not penned inside our own walls waiting for them to come in and pick us off one by one."

"You speak wisely, Governor," Gestian said. Sharzen could tell by the faraway look in his captain's eyes that he was considering the possibilities. "Many would still die, but at least some might live."

"Exactly," Sharzen said. "Can you spread the word,

then? We cannot let our defenses weaken now, but at first light everyone should be ready to make a run for it."

"I will," Gestian promised.

"And at first light," Sharzen added, "I will need a force around me, of course, to guarantee my safe passage to Tanasul. As provincial governor it is vital that I be among the survivors, so that I may negotiate for our interests once we arrive there."

"Certainly," Gestian agreed.

"First light," Sharzen said again, for emphasis. Not that he thought Gestian would forget. But he wanted to make very sure that, when the time came, he had his best men around him as protection.

Most would probably never reach Tanasul, a settlement at least twice Koronaka's size, with a bigger army and better defenses. Sharzen had every intention of doing so. And from there, of striking east for Aquilonia with a larger force, determined to put this place behind him once and for all.

THE *RESTLESS HEART* was anchored where they had expected it to be, its sails furled. No lights shone on board, but as the sun rose it gleamed off the wood of the ship's hull, and Kral could see where to direct the dinghy.

The group had waited inside Tarawa's home while she went out and recruited some able-bodied slaves to help sail the ship. They had left Kuthmet before the dawn and traveled as far as they could before being forced to seek shelter from the most powerful rays of the sun. Once night had fallen, they had continued. At the shore, they had found the dinghy where they'd left it, and climbed in.

The sailors on board reacted with astonishment when the small boat rowed up out of the rising sun, carrying not Gorian and his mercenaries, but Kral, Alanya, Donial, Tarawa, and eight muscular Kushites. When Kral clambered aboard, Allatin strode to meet him, his boots clopping over the deck's boards like the hooves of a horse.

"Who are they?" Allatin demanded, gesturing toward the small boat. His tone was less than friendly.

"My new crew," Kral answered enthusiastically.

"Your crew?" Allatin said. "For what vessel?"

Kral had expected this. "For this one. The *Restless Heart*."

Elonius, the mercenary left on board, put a hand on his sword's hilt and walked to stand at Allatin's shoulder. A couple of the others sailors circled around. Kral stood with his hands resting lightly on his hips, far away from his weapon. He kept his legs spread for balance. If an attack came, it could be from any quarter.

"This is not your ship," Allatin reminded him brusquely.

"Is it yours?" Kral countered. "You gave it up to Gorian easily enough."

"He had—" Allatin began.

"A crew of armed mercenaries?" Kral finished for him. "Gorian's dead, as are his men. But I am not." He ticked his head toward the dinghy. "And I have them."

"Know they aught about sailing?" Allatin queried.

"As much as those mercenaries did, I'll wager," Kral said. "What they don't know, they can be taught. At any rate, your choices are clear. You can't sit here in Stygian waters waiting for Gorian, who will never come. I am sailing with or without you. So you can either come with us or not. I would rather you did, because if I have to kill you, it will take effort and energy better spent putting to sea."

Allatin looked enraged, and his hand closed on the hilt of his cutlass. But then he moved it away without drawing the weapon. "If you're right about Gorian . . ."

"I saw him die."

"Probably murdered him," one of the other sailors said.

"He was killed by Stygian sorcery," Kral corrected. "Which will likely overtake us all if we don't get under way."

"I don't like the sound of that," Allatin said. "What did you get into out there?"

"You would not like the look of it either," Kral said. "But you will see it if we do not settle this now."

Allatin's aggressive posture changed. He looked beaten. Kral could see why he had never captained a ship of his own. A first mate had to be good at taking orders, but a captain had to be able to give them. "Very well," he said. "We all want to be away from here. If what you say is true, then we might as well sail with you as anyone."

"Are we supposed to call a Pict savage 'captain'?"

one of the sailors complained. Kral couldn't tell which had said it. He wished he could have, since ere long that sailor might resent him enough to threaten mutiny.

"Call me whatever you like," Kral said. "As long as you obey my orders, I care not." He went to the side and motioned the others on board. "And my first command is, let's get this ship moving!"

13

AS SHARZEN HAD expected, when the sun broke, the Picts melted back into the trees. Gestian and his men were ready, as promised. They would form a phalanx around Sharzen, who had thrown a few of his most precious possessions, and all the gold he could carry, into leather saddlebags. Outside the walls, the sounds of the Pictish attack had died, and the usual morning sounds the birds made began to be heard.

"They are still out there," Gestian warned. "They have pulled back to rest, but they still watch."

"I know," Sharzen said. He stood with the others outside his private stable. He had selected his sturdiest stallion, and had allotted the rest of his horses to soldiers who had none. "But we will not get a better chance. They will expect us to hold out for at least one more night."

"Probably," Gestian agreed.

"Then of all days, this is the one they will least expect us to make a break for it."

Gestian came closer to him. Sharzen could see how weary the man was—no less so than himself, he was sure. But then, he had not been at the wall most of the night, fighting. He had not slept, but he hadn't been on his feet, either. "I should tell you, Governor," the captain said. "Many of the men do not agree with your plan. They think we should stay and fight, keep the fort until the reinforcements arrive from Aquilonia."

"Those reinforcements would come here to find our headless corpses," Sharzen insisted. "Anyone spared by those savages would wish they had not been."

"I agree," Gestian said quickly. "I just wanted you to know that there is some grumbling in the ranks. Especially from those with families, who feel the women and children merit our protection more than you."

Sharzen had anticipated discontent over his decision. But what could he do? Some of the soldiers had chosen to bring their families to a dangerous place. The border was no place for wives and children. If they tried to remain in Koronaka, they would be committing suicide. At the same time, there were not enough horses for them all to ride, nor enough soldiers to provide them an effective escort to safety. "I am sorry that we will most likely lose some. But they'll stop grumbling when they realize I helped the rest survive."

"Like as not," Gestian said.

"Then let's get on with it," Sharzen said. "To the north gate."

Tanasul was two days' ride to the north, under normal conditions. Scouts had made it in a day by pushing their mounts to the limits, and beyond. With a group this size, and not nearly enough horses available to them—and with Picts waiting to block their way—Sharzen figured the first ones would reach it in two or three days, the stragglers a few days after that, and many not at all.

He mounted his dun stallion, and the guards climbed into their own saddles. At his signal, the gate was thrown open and the horses spurred into sudden action. They burst from the gate and out onto the road in a thunder of hoofbeats, kicking up clouds of dust. *If the Picts aren't watching,* Sharzen thought, *they'll no doubt hear us anyway.*

But as they put more distance between themselves and the fort, he began to feel more confident. The Picts should have been close by, even if they had gone to tend their wounds and catch some sleep. If they hadn't rallied by now, perhaps they had gone all the way back across the Black River. The road was lined with thick pines on both sides, and a soft breeze rustled the branches, making a lulling sound barely heard over the horses' hooves.

Sharzen was about to suggest that they had made it out safely to the rider nearest him, a Poitainian named Martel, when an arrow slammed into Martel's chest, knocking him from his mount.

Another soldier cursed. As one, they put spurs to their horses, raising shields to ward off more arrows.

More of the shafts got through in spite of the shields, and the phalanx surrounding Sharzen was reduced by nearly a third in the space of a few seconds. The governor ducked his head and rode on.

Around him, more soldiers fell.

"Keep riding, Governor!" Gestian yelled, drawing up beside Sharzen. The solid formation of the riders had broken apart.

"I am!" Sharzen returned.

He estimated they had covered less than a mile when the first attack came. With every stride his horse made, he felt encouragement. The Picts had put their effort into surrounding Koronaka—they could not possibly control every mile between there and Tanasul.

Like the soldiers around him, Sharzen drew his sword. He had been a warrior before he became a politician, and he would not allow an ambush to interfere with his escape. He preferred to have others do his fighting when possible—after all, hadn't he done enough of it in his younger days? But he would fight if the need arose.

Now the Picts stopped relying only on their arrows and flooded out from between the trees, bearing spears, axes, and war clubs, screeching their war cries at ear-piercing volume. They leapt from branches, sprang from behind thick trunks, almost seemed to erupt from the earth itself. Their skins were painted blue and dark gray, feathers had been tied to their hair in many cases, and they howled and glared ferociously as they attacked.

Aquilonian soldiers fought back from their horses, or from the ground if their mounts had already been killed. Two of the nearly naked warriors came toward Sharzen, thrusting with spears. He nudged his mount toward one of them, and when the Pict drew away from its slashing hooves he swung the sword in a wide arc, slicing the man across the face. The Pict fell back, blood fountaining from him. Still, the other one tried to lunge at him. Sharzen kicked out with a booted foot, knocking the spearpoint away, and then he leaned out of the saddle and stabbed down into the Pict's upper chest. His sword nearly got stuck in the man's breast-bone, but the momentum of the horse tugged it free.

More of the savage men came, and Sharzen hacked and cut until his shoulders grew weary. He was drenched in blood, most of it belonging, Mitra be praised, to the enemy. Here they had the disadvantage of not being mounted, and the Aquilonians were better armed and ar-mored. Except for those hiding in the trees with bows, the Picts had to show themselves to engage their foes. And once they were engaged, the archers didn't dare shoot.

And then, as abruptly as it had begun, the battle was over. No more Picts appeared from the trees. The mounted Aquilonians continued on their way. Somewhere behind them, those on foot would encounter the remains of the battle and perhaps have another force of Picts to contend with. But ahead, the road seemed clear.

Sharzen blew out a sigh of relief. He was not safe yet, would not feel safe until the gates of Tanasul were barred behind him.

If then. Possibly he would be haunted by Picts until he was in Tarantia itself.

But for now, for this moment, he had a strong steed under him, a cold breeze in his face, and an empty road ahead. He sheathed his sword and rode.

USAM ALLOWED HIMSELF a brief, troubled sleep, and by midday he was inside the abandoned settlement, walking through the empty roads with Klea of the Bear Clan. Buildings were everywhere, mostly constructed of logs or stone. Walls, those that had not burned down, surrounded everything.

"People really choose to live like this?" Usam wondered, waving a hand at the high walls. "Like animals in cages, but of their own making?"

"These do," Klea replied. "When I was carrying on with Kral's work, attacking the wall at night, I could scarcely believe they would go to so much trouble to build a wall that kept them in as much as it kept us out."

"I do not understand how they could breathe in here," Usam said. He tried to picture thick and sturdy Klea clambering over walls and slipping unheard through the brush. She was a Pict, so he did not doubt she could do it. But some Picts were more suited to stealthy attacks than others.

"Maybe they couldn't," Klea said. Klea was aged, and her voice sounded brittle, like dry branches in winter. Usam had not known her long, but the lines in her face had deepened just over the past several weeks, it seemed. She was one of the only two known survivors of the Bear Clan. The youngster, Kral, had disappeared, and Mang was back at the village, ready to take his place as Guardian when the crown was found. "Maybe that is why they ran like frightened dogs as soon as we attacked."

Usam grunted with satisfaction. Klea had a point. The settlers had fought for only two nights. He had thought the siege would last for days and days, and probably cost hundreds of Pictish lives. Perhaps more.

But it had not. They didn't have a firm count yet, but it appeared to be in the dozens, not the hundreds. Now that the battle was over so quickly, the warriors had been instructed to search Koronaka, leaving no spot untouched in the search for the Teeth of the Ice Bear. Since it had been stolen by soldiers from Koronaka, it must have been brought back here. It could have been taken away again, by the settlers who had escaped today, or earlier. But they wouldn't know unless they looked for it.

As they walked, Usam kicked over bits of charred rubble and peered into windows they passed. He tested doors, and if they opened, he left them that way for the search crews. If they did not, he marked an X on them with his knife, to indicate that someone needed to break them down. "And if it is not here?" Klea asked.

"Then we split the force," Usam answered. He had given this a lot of consideration, especially after he'd heard that the settlers had already run away. "Half go to Tanasul, half to Thandara. We do to those settlements as we have done here, and search the ashes for the crown. If we do not find it there, we move to the next two, north and south along the Thunder River, until we do."

"And if it has already been removed to Aquilonia?"

"Then we will have eliminated all the settlements that stand in our way, and we march on Aquilonia herself."

"But . . ." Klea began. Usam gave her a hard stare, and she held her tongue. He was in charge of the Pictish forces and would brook no dissent now that the war had begun. His word had to be law, or the fragile unity of the Pictish clans would unravel.

"The Teeth is the most important thing in all of Pict-dom now," he said. "Until we have it safely in its place, no Picts are safe. We keep fighting until it is returned, or until the Ice Bear comes and claims that which was denied him so long ago—the end of our people."

"It will take some time to search this entire settlement," Klea pointed out. "Even with all these hands."

"It will take what it takes," Usam said. "We can only do what we can do, and nothing more. For the sake of every Pict, though, I pray we find it before it is too late."

DONIAL FOUND TARAWA on deck, standing at the port side, staring off into the night. Stars glimmered overhead, occasionally reflected in the churning, deep water of the sea. Where sea and sky met was darkest black.

"Are you ill?" he asked, concerned.

She turned and graced him with a smile.

"Not at all," she said. "Merely . . . entranced, in a way."

"By what?" Donial could not see much to be entranced by out in the distance. Just the night.

"The sea," she said, indicating it with a wave of her muscular arm. "The sky. I had begun to think that Stygian nights were all I would ever know."

The idea of slavery was repulsive to Donial, and he felt uncomfortable even discussing it. Instead he tried to shift the conversation in a different direction. "Have you ever been at sea?" he asked.

"Not on the deck of a ship," she said. "In a cargo hold, when I was brought to Stygia originally."

"In the hold?" Donial echoed, aghast.

"They were not particularly concerned about our comfort," Tarawa said.

"How many were you?"

Tarawa considered for a moment. "Around ninety, I suppose," she said. "About half of our village, at any rate."

In spite of his initial discomfort, Donial found himself fascinated. Staggered. He caught hold of a ship's line, wrapped it around his wrist as he stood there. "Half? That is incredible."

"But true," she said. She sat down on the deck with her legs crossed, causing Donial to believe she was planning to tell a long story. "My village, called Dugalla, was at the border where vast savanna met thick, deep jungle. Dugalla was little more than a collection of thatched huts where we slept, surrounded by pens where we raised cattle, and fields where we tended some crops. The land provided us with everything else we needed, and we were contented and at peace for the most part. We were not all as primitive as this sounds—my father had been to Aquilonia, as I mentioned, and believed it important that his children know languages and hear about the world.

"Early one morning, I woke and came out of my hut to a strange stillness in the air. Dust motes seemed to hang there, as if suspended on strings. The embers of the previous night's fire glowed without apparent heat or sound. I looked around, and could see a few dogs lying in the early sun, a few people bent over their morning meal. Nothing looked odd, but for some reason I could not shake the feeling that something was wrong.

"And then—" Tarawa's voice broke, and she paused, but only for a second. "And then the stillness was broken by a sudden, brutal attack. Slavers, swarming out of the jungle. They charged us with crossbows, with spears, with swords and axes and other weapons I don't even know the names of. There were several hundred of them, far more than we numbered. Everyone took up arms, but in the end we were too few, and they wore armor that protected them from our weapons."

Donial felt her account affecting him even more strongly than it should have, considering he knew her only slightly, and the rest of her villagers not at all. After a moment's contemplation, he realized it was because her story sounded so much like his own imagination's version of the battle at the Bear Clan village—the battle instigated by his uncle Lupinius, during which his father had been murdered. Likely by that same uncle, he now believed.

"And then what?" he asked, almost dreading the answer.

"They slaughtered many of us," she said simply, betraying no more emotion now that she had reached this part of her tale. "Including my father and two brothers. The rest they locked into chains. For days, they marched us toward the sea. Any who complained were whipped, and after the second infraction, killed. Any who tried to escape or to fight back were killed. Their bodies were released from the chains and left beside the trail.

"Once we reached the coast, we were all loaded into the cargo hold of a ship—crammed in like so many netted fish. Every now and then they threw handfuls of food down to us, usually food that had spoiled so greatly that they would no longer eat it themselves. They gave us buckets of water. We had to ride in that hold with our own wastes and our own dead. We could not see out, did not know if it was day or night, or for how long we traveled. Not terribly long, I imagine, but it seemed like forever.

"Finally, we arrived in Stygia. By now there were barely half of those we had started out with, and of course the rest of us had died back in Dugalla. We were brought to the great slave market of Luxur. There, we were sold, one at a time. Many of the families still together by then were broken up. I was purchased, along with my mother and one remaining brother, and a couple of the other attractive young women of my village, by a representative of Shehkmi al Nasir, although at the time I knew it not. As a master, he was not as harsh as some I have heard of— we females, at any rate, were well fed and housed. But the things he made us do . . . I do not want to even think of them, much less describe them to you. Suffice to say I expect they would repulse you as they do me."

She really was lovely, Donial thought. He hated to think of that wizard's long, bony fingers on her tender dark flesh. "I am . . . I scarcely know what to say, Tarawa. I had never thought it would be so awful."

"I know a little of what you have been through, from Alanya," Tarawa said. "I know that you, too, are orphans. And she told me about Kral, about the Aquilonian attack on his home. So we have all suffered loss, it seems."

"Indeed we have," Donial agreed. "Mine seems almost insignificant compared to yours and Kral's. Alanya and I have a home, an estate, friends."

"And I had . . . well, nothing," Tarawa said. "Acquaintances, among the slaves in Kuthmet. A life I dreaded waking up to every day. Every night when I went to sleep I prayed that it had all been a dream, and I would awaken back in Dugalla. But, of course, that never happened."

"Of course. And so you were willing to help us when we asked."

"Yes," she answered. "More than willing, in fact. Ecstatic would be closer. I do not mind saying that I hate Shehkmi and would do anything to make him unhappy. If I thought we could have killed him, I would have suggested that. But he is too powerful, and his magic would have destroyed us."

Donial felt a sudden chill tickle the back of his neck. "Do you think he will let us get away with stealing from him? Or is he tracking us, even now?"

Tarawa held his gaze for a long moment. "It is not like him to give up easily, I fear."

Which, Donial thought, *is the answer I was afraid of.*

14

THE *RESTLESS HEART*, crewed by the remainder of Captain Ferrin's crew and the Kushites Tarawa had brought along, caught favorable winds and sailed steadily into the setting sun. Shem slipped past off the starboard, then Argos, then they cut to the northwest, past Zingara. Alanya found herself weeping at the glimpse she had of the forested Zingaran coast. The last point of Zingara they would pass, Kordava, at the mouth of the Black River, was where Mikelo had been kidnapped and the place to which he had desperately wanted to return.

They sailed perilously near Zingara's coast. The course had been the subject of considerable debate, with the sailors wanting to go wide, passing around the Barachan Isles with plenty of room to spare. Those isles were full of pirates, all knew, and they didn't want to take the chance of having the ship attacked.

But Kral argued that time was of the essence. Skirting between the islands and the coast would save days, if not weeks, depending on weather and winds out in the open ocean. In the end, Kral won the debate by reminding the others that they had agreed to accept him as the captain and had further agreed to the destination he had insisted upon. That, and the fact that Allatin was frankly afraid of him, and so readily took his side after the slightest intimidation on Kral's part.

So they rushed through the narrow channel between islands and shore, anxious the whole time lest they become the object of assault from one direction or the other. Once clear of the Barachans, they steered out to sea a bit so that instead of passing right by Kordava, they could come at the Black River's mouth from out of the west. The river's mouth was vast, and Kral wanted to avoid close scrutiny from Kordava, Zingara's biggest city, which sat on its eastern edge. The western side was more sparsely settled. Zingarans were often at war with Picts, and Kral wanted to avoid the populated parts of that country if at all possible.

"We'll be at the river soon, Alanya," Kral said. She had been standing on deck, gazing out toward the gap in the thickly wooded banks, with Kordava gleaming whitely on the far side. He had slipped up behind her, as silently as ever, and put a hand on her shoulder. She started, but knew it was him. "It will be dangerous, cutting up through Zingara. Dangerous for a Pict, and for anyone accompanying him."

The plan was to avoid Aquilonia, where Kral was likely still wanted for the supposed murder of her uncle Lupinius, the killing—albeit in self-defense—of an Aquilonian soldier, and the escape from jail that her family friend Cheveray had engineered. Instead they would take the Black River through the Pictish lands to the border of Cimmeria and travel on foot to the village of Taern, where Conor lived. "If I was worried about a little danger, would I have stayed with you this long?" she asked.

Kral chuckled. He looked handsome in the golden late-afternoon sun. Just in the time she had known him, his face seemed to have changed, matured. When they'd met in the forest outside Koronaka, he had definitely been a Pictish boy. Now he was a man, captain of a ship, hardened by tragedy and struggle. His cheeks were narrower, cut by deep crags. Lines had appeared at the edges of his brown eyes. His body, always muscular, was lean, rangy, browned by the sun. "I suppose not," he answered. "But this might be more dangerous yet. We cannot expect to find any friends or allies until we get beyond Zingara's borders, into the Pictish lands."

"Have you talked to Donial about it?" she asked. If her brother chose not to stay with them, she would have been glad. Since their father had died she had felt ever more responsible for him, even though he seemed to believe he had grown up enough to take care of himself.

"You know him," Kral said with a grin. "He's willing to go anywhere, do anything, if he thinks there might be some adventure in it."

Which was exactly what Alanya had been afraid of. "Sometimes I wish he was not so eager," she said.

"You could order him to stay behind," Kral suggested. "He could join up with a trading caravan from Kordava back to Tarantia and wait for us there."

"I could," she admitted. She ran fingers through her hair, which was a dark reddish color now, the ash having been rinsed out. "I could even pay the caravan leader myself and see Donial put aboard a wagon. But do you believe for a moment that he wouldn't be right back with us the next morning?"

Kral nodded. "That sounds like your brother."

"Best to just keep him with us, I guess," Alanya said. "So we can at least keep an eye on him."

"Then keep an eye on him we shall," Kral said. His voice was oddly low, husky. His Aquilonian had improved immeasurably since she had known him. "You know I can make no positive assurances of his safety, or yours. But I will do whatever is in my power—"

"Kral!"

Alanya spun around. It was Allatin, calling to him from the bow.

"Aye?" Kral said.

"We will hold here until dark," Allatin said. "Any closer and we'll be spotted for sure."

"And then at dark, we move in closer?" Kral asked.

"Aye," Allatin said. "We should be able to get a bit

nearer, then you and your friends can take one of the boats the rest of the way."

Kral considered for a moment. "One of your men should accompany us," he suggested. "The dinghy is not suited to the Black. I'll find a canoe, or make one, for that journey. But you'll want your boat back after the three of us have gone."

"I keep telling you, it's four." Tarawa stepped up onto the deck. Donial appeared behind her. Alanya had noticed that the two had been spending a lot of time together since they had set sail.

Alanya was confused. "But . . . I thought you and your friends would make for Kush after this," she said.

"They will," Tarawa corrected. Her strong jaw was set, her posture determined. "As for me, I told you before that I had signed on for the whole journey. Wherever it takes you."

"You have already helped us more than you can know," Kral said. "You owe us nothing."

"You opened my eyes and offered me escape from what I had assumed was to be my lot for as long as I lived," Tarawa countered. "I owe you all. And even if I did not, I would still choose to accompany you if you'd have me. If only to see what the end of this mad quest holds."

"It may hold dangers untold," Kral warned her.

"That matters not," Tarawa said. "There is nothing left for me in Dugalla. And do you think I would have lived long and happily had I stayed in Kuthmet?"

"Not likely," Donial put in. Alanya was not surprised

to hear him add, "We will be glad of your company, Tarawa. Eight hands are better than six."

"Then it is settled," Tarawa said. "Until this is finished, one way or another, I travel with you."

Alanya was glad that Tarawa was so determined. She liked being with Kral and Donial, of course. But she could not deny that having another female with them would be a pleasant change.

"We should make ready to go, then," she said, thinking of her mother's mirror and the Teeth, snug inside its canvas bag in their cabin. "We will not be coming back to this ship again once we leave it."

"I brought nothing with me," Tarawa reminded her, "but the clothing I wore. When I leave, that's what I will take away."

"We can get you some weapons from the ship's stock," Kral assured her. "You do not want to enter Zingara, or the Pictish wilderness, without them."

THE ROAD TO Tanasul was free of Picts, as they all seemed to be farther south, around Koronaka. As a result, Sharzen's journey was unhindered once they had made it clear of the first attack. A distinct coolness in the air as they rode told Sharzen that autumn was passing quickly, giving way to an early winter.

Having sent riders ahead, Sharzen was not surprised to find that his group was expected and that the settlement was on full alert, as ready as they could be for Pictish invasion. At his command, the main gate was opened and his riders allowed entrance. When he dismounted, soldiers were right there to take his horse to a stable to be groomed and fed. Scarcely had he felt solid ground under his boots when a gaunt figure hurried across the open square toward him. Sharzen recognized Pulliam, governor of Tanasul, a man with a dour outlook who found the worst in everything he encountered.

"So you survived after all," Pulliam said as he neared Sharzen. He reached out and clasped Sharzen's arm firmly. "I am glad to see it."

"Did you have any doubts?" Sharzen asked. "I sent riders—"

"Aye," Pulliam said. "But between the time that they left your side and the time you arrived here, any number of disasters could have befallen you."

"True enough," Sharzen said. "You should send riders," he suggested, "to intercept the Aquilonian reinforcements headed for Koronaka, and tell them to come here instead." He pulled his cloak tighter around himself and glanced at the slate-gray afternoon sky. "Cold here. We were attacked once, right after we left Koronaka," he continued, finally answering Pulliam's question. "But only that one time. No sign of the savages after that."

Pulliam tugged on his arm, "Come inside," he said. "You're right, it has become damnably cold here these last few days. But I've hot mulled wine inside. You could probably use some food, as well."

Sharzen had not given food much thought until Pulliam mentioned it. But knowing they were close to Tanasul, he and his guards had ridden through the time they would ordinarily have stopped for lunch. He let Pulliam lead him into a two-story log building. Inside a great room, a fire crackled in a stone fireplace, filling the space with the aroma of woodsmoke. Rustic tables with benches were arrayed in front of it. Pulliam clapped his hands, and a stout servingwoman wearing a gray apron over a rough brown dress came through a doorway. "Wine," Pulliam commanded. "Hot and strong."

He bade Sharzen sit at one of the tables and drew out the bench opposite for himself. With his elbows on the table and his long, narrow hands under his pointy chin, Pulliam looked like an odd collection of angles and corners. He wore his customary frown as he asked, "What happened there, at Koronaka? I've heard only the abbreviated version your riders told me."

"What happened is that our long-standing fear seems to be coming true," Sharzen answered. "Instead of dealing with one clan at a time, the Picts have united, so we had to fight all of them at once. They overwhelmed our defenses, overran our walls. We could not hold them off. Finally, we decided that it would be best to leave the settlement before we were all killed. Those of us you saw come in were only the first group—another, on foot, will follow."

"On foot?" Pulliam echoed. "They'll be slaughtered."

"Perhaps," Sharzen said. "We had not enough mounts for everyone, so they were left to take their chances."

"I saw no women or children with your group," Pulliam pointed out. "Only warriors."

"The men insisted on providing me an armed escort,"

Sharzen said. "The rest of our soldiers stayed behind with the civilians to help protect them."

Pulliam nodded, his eyes locked with Sharzen. They both understood how things worked. Sharzen was not proud of leaving the civilians behind, possibly to die. But he was a realist, and he knew that not everyone could be saved. He knew, also, that it was most important to keep him alive, so that he could share with the other settlements the benefit of his experience in dealing with the Picts. Since the savages had united, he was convinced that the war would be long and bloody, and his wisdom could prove beneficial.

Of course, as soon as possible, he hoped to be back in Aquilonia while others fought it.

KANILLA REY TWISTED his thick lower lip between his fingers, worrying.

He had been unable to make contact with Gorian for some time. And the man had not tried to reach him.

Since he knew his agent had reached Stygia, this led to only one conclusion. Shehkmi al Nasir had defeated Gorian—captured him or killed him outright.

Kanilla Rey had known there was a chance this would happen, of course. He had hoped the mercenaries would be strong enough to resist his Stygian counterpart. But if they weren't—then it might mean that al Nasir had the stone that Kanilla Rey had given to Gorian. The stone that allowed them to communicate with each other.

If al Nasir actually did have the stone, then he would likely be able to trace it back to Kanilla Rey. The connection between it and the much larger rock from which it had come was too strong to be hidden from a sorcerer of Shehkmi al Nasir's abilities.

And when al Nasir knew who had sent armed mercenaries into his home, he would be furious. Kanilla Rey could think of various things al Nasir might do to express his rage, none of them pleasant in the least.

So he had a conundrum on his hands. Did he stay in his longtime home, his sanctum sanctorum, waiting for al Nasir to figure it out? To come for him, or send emissaries? Or did he run?

For that matter, would running help?

He paced the sanctum's floor, gazing at the big rock from time to time as if it might offer some solution. He was doing so when its surface changed, becoming indistinct, then crystallizing into a glassy clarity.

Gorian? Trying to reach him at last?

Kanilla Rey hurried to the big stone, peered into its depths to see if his tool was finally reaching out to him.

But instead of Gorian's face, he saw the scowling visage of Shehkmi al Nasir.

Kanilla Rey clutched for the knife he always wore at his belt, drew it. Its steel could do naught against whatever magical attack al Nasir might hurl at him. The Stygian's penchant for quick revenge was well-known, and Kanilla Rey had no intention of becoming the newest example.

That didn't mean he had to wait here for it to happen.

Clearly Gorian had failed. Now al Nasir knew who was behind the attempt.

Kanilla Rey plunged the blade deep into his own belly, drew it across for several inches, then turned it up and kept carving.

He was still alive when he slumped over, falling across the rock, his body obscuring the image of al Nasir's face. Blood streamed down the sides of the rock.

Just before the blackness of death overtook him, Kanilla Rey thought he heard Shehkmi al Nasir's anguished scream, born of frustration that revenge had been denied him.

Listening to it, Kanilla Rey died with a smile on his face.

15

KRAL PUT HIS powerful shoulders into the rowing, and before the eastern sky had lightened to gray they were heading up the mouth of the Black River. At sea, the current had been with them, steadily helping to push them toward the coast. But as soon as they reached the river's channel, it became a struggle. The Black's strong flow fought him every inch of the way, and even with Tarawa joining in, sweat ran from him in small rivers of its own.

When the sun started to rise, Kral could still see the spires of Kordava over his right shoulder, and he remembered how much Mikelo had wanted to get back to his home city. Instead, the boy's body remained in Stygia, and his spirit had gone to the Mountains of the Dead.

He supposed the fact that he could see the city meant that people in its towers could see the boat. It was a very small craft in a very big river, however, and there were numerous larger ones around, so he wasn't overly concerned about that. Still, he forced himself to row ever harder, just in case. The threat didn't just come from the city, but also from the other boats on the river. Anyone who looked over and saw a Pict rowing into Zingara's interior might cause trouble.

Ahead, the river narrowed. Tall trees lined both banks, interrupted only where the massive gray stones that formed much of the river's bed broke through the surface and jutted up onto the shore. Deeper into Pictish country, Kral knew, the river had carved through granite mountains, and its color against that gray stone earned it the name Black. Here the granite was less prevalent, but there was some.

The water flowed even faster as the banks came together. Kral had been sticking close to the western bank, because it was farther from Kordava. As they made their way upriver, however, he realized they would ultimately have to work their way closer to the center, as occasional villages were perched on both banks. He kept his head down, rowing hard, praying that none of the people they passed paid much mind to the tiny rowboat.

Finally, Kordava disappeared behind a bend in the river, and they pulled the boat to shore in an empty, wooded stretch. Here, Kral, Alanya, Donial, and Tarawa climbed from the dinghy and off-loaded their supplies, leaving only Mialat, one of the *Restless Heart*'s sailors, to row back alone. "The current will aid you," Kral assured the man.

"I know," Mialat replied. Kral knew that, during the night, the *Restless Heart* had drifted closer to shore, so when Mialat reached the sea he would not have as far to row as they had in the darkness. The sailor still had a difficult chore ahead of him, nonetheless.

As did those he left behind. Kral knew how to build a canoe, but it was a lot of work. It would pay off, he knew, once they were traveling upriver through some of the Black's treacherous narrows. There would be rapids as well, which would have to be portaged, and the canoe would be much easier to haul through wild country than the dinghy would have been. He'd watched for one to steal but hadn't seen any likely prospects.

He set the others to making camp while he picked some good trees to skin for their bark. He liked working with pine bark, and there was plenty of it here. He chose strong but supple branches for the thwarts and ribs, and cut down a stouter tree from which to fashion a keel and paddles. A dugout might have been faster to make, but heavier and less maneuverable, so he decided to stick with what he knew best.

While he shaved the bark and prepared it, he instructed the others on how to pick sturdy reeds to tie the branches and shape the downed tree into the parts he needed. That night, exhausted, they bedded down just out of sight of the river. The smells of water and fish and forest filled his nostrils as he drifted off. Donial and Tarawa, he noticed, had spent most of the day working in close proximity, and that night they slept with their heads almost touching. In the morning, Kral snagged a pair of rabbits for breakfast and went back to work.

By the third day, they had a serviceable pine-bark canoe. In other circumstances, Kral would have painted decorations on it, but there was no time for that. He had the crown, but until it was complete, he feared, the threat to his people remained. He was convinced that the missing teeth were in Cimmeria—and even if not, the only man who could tell them where he had sold them was.

"Let's put her in the water and move on," he suggested once everyone had seen the finished boat.

"It's late," Tarawa replied. "The sun will be gone before we know it. Should we not wait until morning?"

"Perhaps we should," Kral said. He knew Tarawa was being practical, not lazy—she had worked as hard as anyone during their trip. "But every day—every hour—might count. If we can get three hours of paddling in before we have to stop for the night, then we should do so."

"I would hate to be on the water when the sun goes down," Donial said. "Without lights, who knows what we might encounter."

"We can put to shore at dusk," Kral said. "That will still give us time to make camp before full dark. Then we can be on our way again with the sun."

The others agreed, and they loaded their things into the canoe, heaviest items in the center and working out from there. Kral knew that a flat-bottomed canoe would have been more stable than the one he had made. But it would not have been as maneuverable, so he counted on his own expertise to keep them upright and afloat. The last thing they needed was to capsize and lose the Teeth of the Ice Bear at the bottom of the Black. Kral was the last one in the canoe—he would be the stern paddler, the one most responsible for determining direction. The others would take turns in the bow. He pushed off the bank, then climbed in, hanging on to both gunwales for stability.

When he had settled down, he let out a sigh. "Here we go," he said. "Pray to whatever gods listen to you that this will be the last leg of our long trek."

Donial, sitting in the bow, raised his paddle from the water. "I'm for that!" he said. "Let's get this done and get back home!"

Easy for him, Kral thought. He had lost his father, but he still had Alanya, and a home.

Kral and Tarawa had none of those things. When this was over, Kral would deliver the Teeth back to the Guardian's cave, where Mang, as clan elder, would take over as the new Guardian. But what then, for him? Stay with Klea at the old village site to protect the cave? Klea was too old to bear children, so if they were to rebuild the Bear Clan, he would need to find another woman. Alanya came to mind. She would never do it, though, never give up Aquilonia and her inherited wealth to live in the forest like a Pict. Tarawa? Not if Donial had anything to say about it. Someone from another clan, then.

Or no one at all. Perhaps the Bear Clan was meant to

be finished, and some other clan would take over protecting the Teeth.

His mind swam with the possibilities. Nothing he
could do about any of it now, though. No firm decisions
he could make. He knew only that if he did not find the
missing teeth in time, none of it would matter.

Clearing his mind of the rest, he put his entire being
to paddling once more. What waited at the end of it all,
none could tell. But he meant to finish it, and to do it
soon.

USAM LED THE Pictish army that went north to attack
the settlement the Aquilonians called Tanasul. His scouts
told him that Bossonians and Taurans had been heading
west to reinforce the settlers, and rumor had it that the
Aquilonian army was marching that way. All of these
things underscored the importance of speed. Not knowing where the Teeth was, and wanting to drive out the
settlers in any event, he was glad that Koronaka had
fallen quickly and prayed that the rest of the settlements
would be the same.

The group that went south had a Loon Clan chieftain
named Jano at its head. Both parties split their forces,
some taking the Black River north or south, others traveling on foot. Two days after completing the fruitless
search for the Teeth at the Koronaka site, Usam stood
among the trees, looking at the walls of Tanasul. The
walls looked sturdy, but so had those at Koronaka. Ar-
mored soldiers patrolled the ramparts, without torches,

but visible anyway in the pale moonlight. More than there had been at Koronaka, but he had expected that. The assault on Koronaka had taken the settlers by surprise, even though they were the ones who had initially broken the delicate peace that existed in the region. Once that battle had been joined, others would be anticipated.

Still, he expected the settlers to underestimate just how many Pictish warriors there were, as well as the fire that burned in their guts for victory. This was not just a military campaign; it was a battle for the very survival of his people.

The ground under Usam's feet was frozen and crunchy. He did not object to the cold—Picts lived largely outside in every kind of weather. But he was surprised by it for that same reason. He knew what to expect of the weather, month in and month out. He knew it was subject to variation from year to year, but for the most part, it followed certain long-standing patterns. And always, *always,* winter had been preceded by an autumn of some duration or other.

Not this year, it seemed. Early autumn had been warm. Then, with what seemed no transitional time at all, it had turned cold. He did not know what it meant, but he didn't like it.

The cracking of a downed branch, behind him. Usam spun, raising his newly acquired spear. But it was only Galok, a warrior of the Eagle Clan. He was a broad-shouldered man with short, bandy legs and a deep chest. Eagle feathers dangled from his long, dark hair, bumping into the wolfskin cloak draped over his shoulders. He smiled at Usam, showing uneven yellow teeth. "Usam," he said as he approached. "Are they ready for us?"

"They think they are," Usam said. "But they are mistaken."

Galok laughed dryly. "We should have done this years ago. We should never have let them build those settlements in the first place."

"Agreed," Usam said. "But we were not making those decisions, you and I. Our forefathers believed them when they said they wanted to live in peace. Ask the Bear Clan if they meant it."

Galok chuckled again. "Which one? Mang, or Klea?"

Usam smiled briefly, but the loss of an entire clan was nothing to laugh about. Pointing toward the wall, he said, "Many guards on duty, see? They know, because of what happened at Koronaka, that we will attack during the night. They think if they patrol without torches, we will not see them."

"Because the senses of civilized men are dulled by the way they live," Galok surmised. "So they do not understand how much better ours are."

"Possibly. In this case, they will be disappointed."

"In what way?" Galok asked.

"They will wait all night for us to attack," Usam said. "Tiring themselves—their best warriors, who are undoubtedly the ones on the walls tonight. By morning they will decide that we will not come until the sun sets again. Their best warriors will go into their buildings, to their soft beds, possibly after gorging themselves on their rich meals. The weaker ones will take up positions on the walls, knowing they are not in danger from us until dark."

"So we will attack at sunrise?" Galok speculated.

"No," Usam said with a grin. "We will wait. Let the soldiers who have been on the wall all night get their meals and fall fast asleep. Let their replacements decide that they are in for a long day on the walls, waiting for an attack that never comes. There is no particular reason we have to attack with the rising sun, or the setting one. In the past we have done so, because it functions as a signal that warriors on all sides can see. But now, there are so many of us, we can pass the word, one to the next."

Galok laughed once more. "So we attack at midmorning, when they least expect us."

"That's correct," Usam said. "Spread the word, now. We only want it to be a surprise to their forces, not to ours."

Nodding, Galok started to walk away. "I am glad you were made the war leader of our people," he said. "I hope Jano is as clever, at Thandara. The sooner our lands are rid of these interlopers, the better."

16

SHEHKMI AL NASIR let the fire burn brightly. It was contained within a circle drawn on the stone floor of his inner sanctum—drawn in the blood of a young goat kept specifically for that purpose. Once the fire reached waist height, al Nasir dropped certain powdered herbs into it, making the flames change colors and spit toward the ceiling. Another powder turned them green and gave off a foul, sulphuric odor.

When he felt the time was right, he doused the whole thing with a handy pail of water. The fire sizzled; thick gray smoke billowed toward the ceiling.

Perfect.

He spoke a few words and tossed two handfuls of yet another powder, this one made from the dried venom of a particular species of cobra, into the smoke. A patch of it, where the powder had struck, turned smooth, almost glassy. The gray color dissipated. It had become a kind of window. But instead of a window showing what was on the other side of the room, it showed a scene from what must have been hundreds, if not thousands, of miles away.

No longer in Stygia, at any rate.

He saw a dark river, its water almost black in color, which he assumed to be from the gray stone channel it ran in. On that river, he saw a plain brown canoe with four people in it. Only one of those did he recognize. The lovely Tarawa, who had vanished some days back, and who he assumed had been involved in the theft of his Pictish treasure because of the timing of her disappearance.

Al Nasir smiled. He would reserve a special punishment for her. One that would take days and days, making her beg for the sweet release of death. The others could be killed quickly or slowly, as circumstances dictated. They were common thieves, he supposed, and nothing better could be expected of them. He had been surprised that they had come in the company of mercenaries, but not that they had abandoned the corpses of their fellows so readily. Mercenaries and that young boy who stank of the sea.

But they had taken his crown, and so they would be dealt with.

Not right away, though. They had an apparent goal, a destination. Al Nasir had to assume that they were on the trail of the missing teeth, else they would have taken the crown straight to Kanilla Rey and not gone to the trouble of building themselves a canoe and paddling up a wild river. Unless they were not working for Kanilla Rey after all, as he knew the dead fighting men had been. Or unless they had some way of knowing that the Aquilonian mage had killed himself to avoid al Nasir's vengeance.

If they thought they could find the teeth, he was more than happy to let them. If they turned out to be unsuccessful—or if, unlikely as it seemed, he was wrong in his judgment of their course—he would have them killed then.

In the meantime, he would have to prepare some acolytes for another ocean voyage. This time they would be more wary of failure, he wagered.

Before he let the image fade away, he listened to it, sniffed it. He could not hear things like conversations, could not smell the odors of river water or unwashed bodies. But he could, nonetheless, collect impressions about the place he observed. When he was satisfied, he waved a hand at the smoke window, and it vanished.

The Black River, he had decided. Heading north. Into the Pictish lands, no doubt. It made sense—a Pictish crown, and one of those in the boat appeared to be a Pict as well.

He would, of course, keep an eye on them. But it was a starting point.

THE SECOND DAY on the river the group encountered the first set of rapids.

Alanya looked at the water with a worried eye. It had started flowing faster, showing whitecaps. She had seen rapids before, but never from a tiny boat trying to force its way against the current. She didn't want to sound worried, but she had to know. "Are you sure we can do this, Kral?"

"Of course," Kral answered confidently. "This one's easy. Wait until we reach Dead Elk Narrows. That is where you can worry."

"So you have been here before?" Tarawa asked.

"Not exactly," Kral said. He had never been inside Zingara's borders before the *Restless Heart* dropped them off, and they had not yet passed into the Pictish wilderness. They were well into Zingara now, though past the most populous parts, and had not seen another boat since early morning.

"Then how do you know?" Donial wondered.

"I have heard stories of the Black River all my life," Kral explained. "None of them told of treacherous waters this deep inside Zingara. So I have to believe that this will only be some minor whitewater and nothing terribly difficult to navigate."

Alanya's concern was not completely alleviated by that explanation. Just because no one had told Kral stories of this spot did not mean it wasn't trouble. How many of his friends or family had ever traveled down the river as far as Zingara, after all? It did not sound like a lot, from things he had said previously.

So she continued to feel trepidation as the little boat made its way upriver into increasingly turbulent waters.

The whitecaps were higher and more frequent now, splashing her inside the canoe. Kral still held his position in the tiny craft's stern, helping to keep the canoe upright against the rough water, while Tarawa paddled in the bow.

Within minutes, she could hear a dull roar as the once-placid river turned into a thundering monster. Kral and Tarawa increased the pace of their paddling. The canoe shuddered and shook. Alanya hoped it would hold together, since it had been crafted so quickly. What if it had needed more time to set? They could easily swim to shore, but her mother's mirror was in a pouch on the canoe's floor, as was the crown they had traveled so far to claim.

A surge pushed against the bow, turning the canoe almost sideways in the river. Kral shouted at Tarawa to stop paddling, and he jammed his own paddle in the water and held it firm, slowing the sideways movement. Then he bade Tarawa paddle in a wide, sweeping motion on the canoe's left side. Working together in this way, they managed to bring the canoe back to its proper orientation. But they had lost momentum, and even though they paddled hard, the craft barely seemed to move forward against the rushing current.

"Perhaps we should get out and carry it," Alanya said.

"Not yet," Donial countered, apparently speaking for Kral and Tarawa, both too involved in their effort to talk. "We make progress still."

She had noticed that Donial had been disagreeing with her more frequently lately. Well, that was not quite accurate, she amended mentally. As a little brother, he had always been somewhat argumentative. If she had said the sky was a lovely shade of blue today, he might have claimed that it was a sinister cerulean, instead. But recently, his disagreements had been over matters of greater substance, and expressed freely, with less emotion attached. Perhaps it was just a function of his growing up or a reaction to the stresses of the journey.

Or maybe he was showing off for Tarawa. A combination of all three, most likely.

Still, as the water became choppier, the current yet more forceful, she worried. Kral seemed determined to beat the river. He jammed his paddle into the water, tugged it back, raised it out, and plowed it back in with what looked to her like anger. All she could see of Tarawa was the girl's back, her shoulders broad, her arms working feverishly, mechanically, as she tried to match Kral's urgency.

Finally, they rounded a wooded bend and saw the source of the thunder. A short waterfall. Really, just a collection of massive granite boulders over which the river spilled, dropping about a dozen feet to the lower surface, where it landed with a white crash before continuing downstream.

"We cannot . . . cannot possibly paddle up that," Alanya pointed out.

"You are right," Kral said, breathing hard with the effort of paddling. "Time to portage."

He turned the canoe toward the west bank—it slipped back downriver as they went—and pulled for shore. By the time they reached it, all were soaked to the skin by water splashing up over the gunwales, and the belongings stuffed into the bottom of the canoe were equally wet. At the bank, Tarawa jumped out first, grabbing the bow with both hands and dragging it up onto a pebbled strip of sand. The others followed her out, then removed their various tied-down belongings, shaking the river water from them as best they could. Finally, Donial and Kral lifted the canoe and turned it over to dump out the water that had collected inside.

Kral seemed almost reluctant to set the canoe back down on the ground. "I know time is important," Alanya said. "But we really should rest for a short while, shouldn't we? It will do us no good to kill ourselves with exhaustion before we get to Cimmeria."

Kral relented unhappily. "I suppose you're right," he said, lowering himself to a fallen tree. "But only a short break. I fear that time is running out even as we travel. I could not tell you why I feel that way . . . but I do."

"Every mile we put between us and Stygia makes me happy," Tarawa said. "The quicker the better, for me."

"I know," Alanya replied. "For me, too. I do not mean to nag, but you are both working so hard. When we get back in the river it's my turn to paddle for a while. Me and Donial."

"That's right," Donial added. "We have watched you two workhorses long enough."

Tarawa laughed and flashed her brilliant smile his way. "So I look like a horse to you?"

"Not at all," Donial backtracked. "You look . . . like

a lovely girl who has just come out of the bath. With her clothing on."

"Would you have it any other way?" Tarawa teased.

"Perhaps not here in front of the others," Donial suggested with a wicked grin. "But in private . . ."

"In private you'd see just what you do now," Tarawa assured him.

Alanya wondered if she meant it. Their banter was definitely flirtatious. But Tarawa had probably had enough of the touch of men for a while, if not for a lifetime, judging from what little she had said about her service to al Nasir.

Kral smiled at their exchange, then nodded his assent to Alanya's suggestion. "Very well," he agreed wearily. "You two take over on the other side." He closed his eyes and relaxed his limbs for a while. Alanya shivered from the soaking she had taken, and the cold air on her flesh as it dried. But she knew the chore of hauling the canoe and all their belongings through the woods and up the slope, to get around the boulders obstructing the river, would warm her back up again. After that, the effort of paddling the boat would likely keep her that way.

She closed her own eyes. Her muscles, she realized, were bunched up and tense from the encounter with the falls. She didn't feel like sleeping, but she wanted to relax them before they got under way again. The day was far from over, and they had miles yet to go.

17

SHARZEN SAT IN Pulliam's office, waiting.

Waiting.

The governor of Tanasul had been hospitable enough. Sharzen's belly was full, he had wine or mead when he wanted it, and he had been offered his choice of several women with whom to while away the hours. The office was kept warm by a steady fire, and the two couches in there were comfortable. Pulliam himself was out at the moment, checking on the troops, but when he was around his conversation was interesting and wide-ranging. Every day, reinforcements arrived— not the promised Aquilonian army, but Gundermen, Poitainians, Bossonians, Taurans, and the like, coming singly or in pairs or in small groups. Coming to offer their swords against the battle they all knew was coming.

Even the rest of the group from Koronaka—about half the size of the original group, he noted sadly—had shown up.

With all the new arrivals milling around, looking for housing, training with the troops, Tanasul looked like a busy settlement. But Sharzen knew it was all just part of the waiting.

The Picts would be here soon, he knew. Pulliam's soldiers had seen shadows moving about in the trees. Bird sounds had been interrupted, and less than an hour ago someone had reported seeing a flock take off from their treetop perches as one, a sure sign that something had disturbed them. Sharzen was convinced he knew what it had been.

He wished something would happen. The Aquilonian army to arrive. The Picts to just attack, to get the waiting over with. Anything would be better than this anticipation, this unending dread.

From outside, he heard some kind of commotion. *It's begun,* he thought, lurching unsteadily to his feet. Perhaps he had consumed a bit too much wine. He tried to shake off the effects as he fought his sword from its scabbard and headed for the door.

Before he reached it, however, the door was thrown open and four soldiers muscled a nearly naked Pict warrior inside with his hands tied or shackled behind his back. The man looked like some kind of wild beast, snarling and hissing, wrenching his shoulders in every direction to try to toss off the soldiers gripping them. Pulliam followed them in, glaring at the prisoner. He pointed toward an empty corner of the big room. "There!" he shouted. "Put him there!"

The soldiers hauled their prisoner to the indicated corner and slammed him against the wall, face-first. The Pict slowly turned back toward the room, blood running from his nose and lips. He pressed his back into the corner and sank to the floor, staring ferociously at his captors.

Pulliam hoisted himself up to his full height, which was not very much taller than the Pict, and strode across the room. He stood just out of the Pict's reach, Sharzen noted, and the soldiers surrounded the savage with swords and a halberd. "Now, you," Pulliam said. "Tell us what your people are up to. I know you plan to attack us, but when? How? How many are you?"

The Pict just glowered at him. "Perhaps he speaks no Aquilonian," Sharzen suggested.

Pulliam kicked at the cornered man, hitting a hand the Pict raised in self-defense. "He speaks it!" Pulliam shot back. "He just doesn't want to help us." He drew his own sword and turned back to the prisoner. "But he will." He held the tip of his blade out toward the Pict. The man was already pressed into the corner, with no place to escape to, so when Pulliam's blade scraped across his cheek, just beneath his right eye, he had nowhere to turn.

"Well?" Pulliam demanded.

The Pict still did not answer. He slowly raised one hand and wiped blood off his chin and lips. Pulliam's blade wavered as if the very steel grew nervous at the proximity of the Pict's hand. The Pict's fierce dark eyes blazed with fury.

"I'm waiting," Pulliam said. "But in another thirty seconds, I shall put out your eye. So you had better tell me what I want to know."

Still, the Pict only sat and stared. His hand had gone higher now, tugging through his mad tangle of dark hair. He did not look, to Sharzen, particularly scared. Angry, yes. Perhaps even vengeful. But not frightened.

Which, Sharzen realized, scared *him* just a little.

Pulliam pressed against the man's cheek with the point of his blade, cutting the flesh there, and inscribing a line up toward his right eye. The Pict watched it coming with interest but without evident fear. Sharzen found himself amazed and impressed by the savage's cold disregard for his impending mutilation.

Another second passed. The blade came closer to the Pict's eye. Then, faster than Sharzen could even follow, the Pict moved. He grabbed the flat of Pulliam's blade and wrenched the sword from the governor's hand. Before Pulliam could even react, the savage had spun the sword around so the grip ended up in his fist. Evidently deciding that a disarmed Pulliam posed little threat, the Pict ignored him and slashed out at the nearest of the guards, slicing through the flesh of his sword arm. The one wielding the halberd jabbed at the Pict with his long-handled weapon, but the Pict snatched the halberd's shaft and tugged the soldier off-balance, onto his outthrust sword. The soldier made a choking noise and fell backward as the Pict yanked his blade free.

The two uninjured soldiers both stabbed at the prisoner with their swords, but the savage blocked one of the attacks and ignored the second, which raked across his naked ribs. He charged, heedless of the soldiers' greater familiarity with swords or their armor, slashing with his stolen blade as if it were a stick or club. The sheer ferocity of his attack drove the soldiers back, and though they were unable to land another blade on him, he drew blood again and again. The soldier who had been cut first tried to help, but his sword arm was weakened and when the Pict's blade slammed into his, he let go of the sword and it flew away, bounding off the ceiling before clattering to the floor. Pulliam dove for it.

Sharzen's own sword had been in his hand since before they had entered the room, and he realized that it was still there. He had not intended to interfere, but at this point it was beginning to look as if the Pict would escape if he didn't—maybe even killing him in the process. He started toward the fray. Before he could make it across the room, however, two more soldiers were down, one spraying blood from his throat and the other writhing on the floor, in serious pain. The last one was barely upright. The Pict made short work of him. Pulliam stood there, the reclaimed sword in his trembling hand.

"Pulliam, move!" Sharzen shouted. Pulliam's head twitched, and he seemed belatedly to understand Sharzen's urgency. He began to back away from the prisoner. At the same time, Sharzen advanced, blade raised, ready to meet the threat if the Pict got through the last soldier. "Sound an alarm, Pulliam!" Sharzen said. "Call for help!"

As if a string had been cut, Pulliam reacted, turning his back on the Pict and preparing to run. But the Pict took advantage of the moment to plunge his weapon into Pulliam's back, and the point burst, dripping with gore, from the governor's shallow chest. Pulliam made a sucking sound and clutched uselessly at his breast, then lurched forward as the Pict shoved him off the blade with a bare foot on his lower back.

Now only Sharzen stood between the Pict and the door. The Pict showed him gnashing teeth, as a trapped animal might. He advanced, his sword making short, cutting motions. Sharzen considered his plight for a moment, then stepped aside.

Outside, the place was crawling with soldiers. No doubt some were already on the way, having heard the clash in their governor's office. Better to let the soldiers stop him. With Pulliam dead, Tanasul would need experienced leadership. The Pict stopped before him, looked him in the eye, and whispered, "Coward," then dashed out the door.

Sharzen went right behind him, screaming at the top of his voice. "He's loose!" he called. "Pict on the loose! Stop him—he's murdered Pulliam!"

Soldiers came running at Sharzen's cries, but the Pict was already a blur, racing across the open square away from the office. At the nearest gate, three soldiers made ready for the Pict's arrival. They stabbed at him when he reached them, but he let out a horrendous war whoop and sliced through them as if they were mere children playing at war. Before the nearest other soldiers could reinforce their comrades, the Pict was working open the great wooden bolt that held the gates closed.

And from the other side, pressure on the wooden gates caused them to bulge inward where they met. Soldiers reached the Pict and skewered him against the log gate, but too late. The gates pressed inward and a swarm of dark bodies pushed through, overwhelming the soldiers with spears and clubs. Their triumphant war cries echoed throughout the log walls of Tanasul, drowning out the shouts of alarm from the Aquilonians. Sharzen stood in the doorway of Pulliam's office, carnage behind him, and watched as the Picts flooded in.

Soldiers streamed toward the square now, many tugging on armor as they came. Sharzen knew that Pulliam had put his best men on the night watch, and that now they were sleeping in preparation for the coming night's expected assault. At the sound of the Pictish incursion, they were being roused, but they were unprepared, sluggish. The Aquilonians were cut down by the fiercely energized Picts, like so much tall grass falling before a scythe.

Sharzen retreated inside the office. The stink of death assailed him here, but at least he was safe for the moment from the melee outside, though the sounds of combat rattled his nerves. Hazarding a glance out the door he saw that the stream of Picts rushing in through the gate continued, like water through a burst dam. Shouts from the parapets alerted him to the fact that arrows were flying as well, slaying many of the soldiers on guard there.

Sharzen sat down heavily on one of the couches.

Nearby, a soldier whom the Pictish prisoner had only wounded but not killed made gurgling noises as he tried to draw air into his damaged lungs. Sharzen found himself wishing the man would be silent, even though he knew it would mean the soldier's demise.

Oddly, he found himself recalling an incident from his youth. He'd been raised on a sprawling farm outside Poitain, and on this one occasion in his ninth year, he had gone wandering in the fields. As afternoon wore into evening, he found himself far from home. A strange noise had drawn his attention to a patch of forest near the fields, and, torn between curiosity and outright terror, he had forced his young legs to carry him there.

After searching for several minutes, Sharzen found a den of some kind—a hole about ten inches across, dug at the base of a large bush. The sound, which he had decided was a whimper of pain, came from there. He tried to peer inside, but the sun was dropping fast and this part of the forest was lost in shadow. He barely dared to get closer—what if it was an injured animal who would attack him? He had no weapons, nothing with which to defend himself.

But the noise continued, like nothing he had ever heard. *What if it is some kind of fairy?* he thought. A magical being who would reward his help? He'd heard tales of such things before, and he would hate to miss his chance if that was the case.

Looking rapidly about him, he found a stick about as long as his arm and big around as his wrist. He returned to the hole, or den, from which the high-pitched, squealing noise came louder than ever. Kneeling before it, he prodded with the stick. Whatever was inside gave a sharp screech, as if he had hurt it. He poked again. Another screech, and the thing inside seemed to snatch at the stick. Sharzen pulled it free, glanced at the sky. Darker and darker. He didn't want to be here with whatever was down there in full dark, he knew.

Back on hands and knees, he tried once again to see into the den. "Hello?" he asked, his voice quaking with anxiety. "Are you a fairy?"

Only the agonized whimpering answered him.

"Something else, then? A troll?" He tried to remember what other types of creatures dwelled in the woods, in the stories his parents had told him. Part of him knew those stories weren't true, but to admit that would mean giving up a precious part of his childhood, and he was not yet ready to do that. "Some sort of boggart?"

Only the whimper.

Finally, he had clapped his hands over his ears and run out of the forest, back through the broad fields toward home. He had been careful to stay away from that part of the farm for many months, and when he finally worked up the courage to look again, winter's rains had collapsed the hole.

He'd felt a powerful self-loathing then. He had exhibited undeniable cowardice. He might have been able to save something's life, even if it was just the injured animal he suspected it had been. If not, he might have been able to end its agony with the stick. Instead, he had done nothing, had run away.

He determined then, as a boy of ten summers, that he would become a brave man. A soldier, a warrior, a leader of others. And he had done those things, swallowing his fears, pushing aside his moments of insecurity, the late-night panics.

And now? Now he was hiding in a dead man's office, watching a brave, wounded soldier breathe his last, doing nothing to help the man because it might call attention to the fact that he was in here.

So, Sharzen thought. *The truth of it comes out at last, all these decades later.* If bravery meant facing things one feared and doing them anyway, then he had been brave for a long time. But in the end, as he neared what would be the twilight years of his life, his real nature pushed to the fore again.

Born a coward, he thought. *And you'll die one.*

But not here, not now. In a soft bed in Aquilonia, surrounded by round, yielding feminine bodies. And only when age had weakened his limbs, stolen his strength and sapped his will.

Because Sharzen was not only a coward. He was also a survivor. If he had only been a coward, he would have died a hundred times by now. The fact that he yet lived was testament to his most powerful trait. It had pulled him through dozens of close scrapes before, and it would this time as well. He just needed to apply his intellect and instincts to the problem at hand.

Cautiously, he went back to the door and took another look. Measuring his chances.

He would stay right where he was for a while longer,

he decided. The tide of battle may have been turning, but he wasn't confident of that yet. A little more time.

He came back into the office, sat down again.

Thankfully, the noisy soldier had died.

18

THE BORDER BETWEEN Zingara and the Pictish lands was not marked in any way. Kral knew that if they had been traveling on the road, it would have been well marked—on the Zingaran side, not the Pictish one. Picts cared little for the borders demarcated by men. They were used to being able to wander at will, and the only borders that mattered to them were natural ones: the coastline or the nearly impenetrable mountains that separated them from Vanaheim.

But here on the river, the borderline came deep in the Rabirian mountains. Kral had no way to know precisely when they had crossed over. He assumed that they had when he could see the top of the seemingly endless forest canopy, instead of merely more and higher peaks.

The Rabirian mountains were tall, forbidding mountains whose peaks were blanketed with snow. The Black River sliced through canyons with steep vertical walls that seemed to keep the sun out altogether. In those canyons, the only sound that could be heard was the pounding of the river as its course cut deeper and deeper into the hard granite surface. No birds flitted about down here, no insects buzzed. The air was bitingly cold, the river frozen at the edges. Frequently, they had to carry the canoe up bare rocky slopes where the water tumbled down with ferocious power.

At the top of one such rise, Kral paused and pointed through a slender gap in the rock walls. "Look," he said to no one in particular. "That is my homeland."

"I thought Kush had a lot of trees," Tarawa said. "Does the sun ever reach the earth there?"

Kral chuckled. "Yes, it does. We have clearings, and hilltops bare of trees. But the forests are life to us, and sacred."

Donial had put on all his clothing and wore a fur cloak over everything, and still he shivered. "I never thought I would be so happy to see Pictish lands again," he said. "Perhaps it will not be so cold there."

"It does get cold," Kral acknowledged. "But seldom like this."

"Then we should get down there before we freeze to death," Alanya said.

"I'm for that," Tarawa said. Like Donial, she was so bundled up Kral could barely understand how she could

move. Even with all that on her, however, she still managed to take her turn rowing.

"Why do we stand here talking, then?" Kral asked.
"The sooner we move on, the sooner we reach warmer
climes."

They launched the canoe into calmer waters and paddled toward home. Even more rapidly than he had anticipated, they left the Rabirians behind, and welcome sun
shone down on them once more. Before long, however,
the tall trees arched over the river, shielding it from the
sun's rays. Kral was surprised to realize that it was no
warmer here than it had been in the hills. The leaves had
turned brown or fallen; early frosts had killed underbrush that should still have been green and thriving this
time of year.

That evening, they beached the canoe and built a
roaring fire beside the river. Kral was no longer worried
about the smoke alerting anyone. The only people who
would see were fellow Picts, and at this point he would
be glad to encounter them.

But none came to see who had started the fire. In
the morning, while the others slept, he rose early and
walked away from the river, inscribing a wide circle. He
found, nestled against the base of a hill, an abandoned
campsite where it appeared that a clan had lived, at least
for a time. The fire pits were cold, the huts empty. He
looked around, kicked over blown leaves, hoping to find
some clue as to where they might have gone. Fear rushed
through him—had the Aquilonians attacked this clan,
too? But he saw none of the bodies or burned-out rubble

that would indicate that. The people had simply left.

When he got back to his own camp, the others were up, getting ready for the day's voyage. Alanya gave him a concerned look. "Where have you been?" she inquired.

"I thought perhaps there would be a clan's village around here," he explained. "And I found one, but empty. Not for too long, I'd wager—weeks, perhaps. No longer."

"Is it normal for them to move like that?"

"Some clans are more nomadic than others," Kral replied. "The Bear Clan always stayed on our hill, because we were protecting the Guardian's cave. But some move depending on the season, to places where the hunting or fishing might be better."

"So this could have been something like that."

"Could have been," Kral agreed. "But something about it made me think they left quickly. It's just odd, that's all."

"Well, we should leave quickly, too," Alanya reminded him. "We have a long way to go."

Kral agreed, and they set off within a few minutes. But all that day, he watched and listened for signs of his people near the Black. And all that day, he heard none, saw no one. The Pictish wilderness seemed as empty as if it had never been inhabited in the first place.

Kral didn't understand it.

But he knew he didn't like it.

"HOW GOES THE battle?"

Usam sat before a fire while Mara wrapped strips of

cloth around his wounded shoulder. Now that the attack
had begun, he did not worry about the settlers seeing
their fires. In fact, he encouraged the lighting of many
of them, to let the Aquilonians know how outnumbered
they were. Besides, the numerous fires helped dispel the
chill that had gripped the land. Women and children had
established camps near the settlements to tend to the
warriors, who had to be free of worrying about food and
shelter so they could devote their attention to battle. In
these camps, they kept the fires burning day and night.
Thousands of Picts—most of the population of his
race—were huddled around these fires, or else near no
doubt similar ones outside Thandara.

"Harder than the last," he admitted to his wife. "Many
of our warriors got inside the gate right at the first, as I
told you. But they got the gates closed again, and those
brave ones are no doubt dead, or else prisoners. We will
wear them down, make no mistake. But I had hoped for
another easy victory. I fear this sudden winter might portend the approach of the Ice Bear, and unless we can find
that crown quickly, all our efforts might be for naught.
The Aquilonians will find themselves—such of those
as survive—holding sway over an empty, ice-choked
wilderness."

Mara clucked at him and pulled the bandages tight
enough to make him wince. "I have never heard you so
ready to admit defeat, husband."

"Not defeat," he corrected. "Just worry. We know the
Ice Bear stirs, because the Teeth has been missing so
long. We know this weather is unseasonable. I am not

ready to lay down arms and die. I simply accept the fact that we need fast victories, here and at Thandara. And we need to hope that the crown has not made it farther afield than that."

Mara held a cup of some pungent brew made from local leaves to his lips, and he drank, swallowing rapidly so as not to taste it more than necessary. "This will help you heal, Usam," she said. "You are ready to continue the battle—at least, as ready as I can make you."

Usam put a hand on her shoulder and used it to steady himself as he rose. He winced again. An Aquilonian arrow had pierced the shoulder. He had tugged it through, but the pain had been excruciating, and he'd lost a lot of blood. Now he raised his arm, lifting his hand high over his head, moving it in a slow circle. It hurt, but it functioned.

Pain, he could live with.

It was as nothing compared to the agony he meant to inflict on the settlers inside those walls.

"I wait for news from Thandara," he said as he buckled on his girdle. "If it comes today, send for me at the wall."

FAR TO THE north, the Vanir legend Grimnir wove his powerful magic. Tall as two of the biggest Picts ever born, big around as the trees that gave them shelter, Grimnir knew he was feared and hated, and he worked to encourage both. Grimnir the invincible, men called him. Grimnir the immortal. When they spoke his name, they did so in whispers, lest they call his yellow-eyed gaze upon themselves. He shook his head, the mad tangle of red hair threaded with silver, and roared his laughter at the oppressive skies.

Grimnir had reason to hate the Cimmerians. And while he often chose to express that hate by smashing Cimmerian heads with his great warhammer, he also knew the value of more wide-ranging assaults.

So he had called upon Ymir, god of the northern people, Aesir and Vanir alike, creator of the world and all its beings. Grimnir was said, according to those who saw him, to resemble the frost giant, with his feral eyes and frost-rimed beard and massive stature. And Ymir, working through him, had granted him his boon. A storm blew down from the farthest northern reaches, a storm the likes of which Cimmeria had never known. Steel, brittled by the severe cold, snapped like dry twigs. Rushing streams froze solid, resisting all efforts to melt them for drinking water. Fires were extinguished by wind and driving sleet. Ice blanketed all the land.

Vanirmen took advantage of the storm to stage raids into Cimmeria, which was what Grimnir had intended. If the storm affected regions south of Cimmeria, that was no concern of Grimnir's. He only hoped to paralyze his enemy so that the Vanir could finally vanquish them once and for all.

He snapped an icicle from his beard and put it into his mouth. He barely remembered his own childhood, but he remembered having done that, sucking on icicles, from his earliest days. He had been born of the cold, for the cold. Tasting it, he threw back his giant head and laughed again.

THE BLACK RIVER led ever north, forming the natural boundary between the Pictish wilderness and the Westermarck, flowing from a source near the Cimmerian border. Every night they camped on the west side of the river, the Pict side. Every day, they watched and listened for signs. Donial knew that with each passing day and no trace of the Picts, Kral grew more worried. Perhaps the tragedy that the loss of the Teeth of the Ice Bear was supposed to portend had already happened. Even Donial, who knew the region only slightly, was mystified and concerned by the quiet.

At night they built fires to chase away the bitter cold. Donial sat next to Tarawa on one of these nights, both huddled under their cloaks, both shivering in spite of the leaping flames.

"I . . . can't believe how cold it is," she complained. "I have never imagined such cold. How can people live here?"

"It is not usually like this," Donial said. "In the summer it is pleasant enough, with warm days and cool nights. This seems unnatural to me. Do you think Shehkmi al Nasir could be behind it?"

"I would never put anything past him," she said. "But I do not see his hand in this. What would it profit him?"

"If not he, then who?" Donial wondered. "Why would the weather be so strange?"

"I know not," Tarawa said. The dancing firelight reflected in her wide brown eyes, liquid with fear. "I do not think of myself as a weak person, Donial. But I worry that this cold will kill me before we reach our goal."

"I would not allow that," Donial said.

Tarawa smiled at him. "You have dominion over the weather? Then bring back the sun."

Donial shrugged. "Would that I could. If it were in my power, I would bring the sun out to warm you, and I would bring back the Picts to ease Kral's mind."

"And for yourself?" she asked. "For your sister? Anything?"

"Short of being able to bring back the dead, there is not much that we need," he said. "We have a home. We have each other. Whenever we get back to Tarantia, we will have family business interests to attend to. I guess all we need is an end to this quest."

"And yet, here you are," Tarawa pointed out. "You have stayed with Kral voluntarily, when you could have gone home at any time to tend to your affairs."

Another shrug. "Kral is our friend," he said. He tried to see into the shadows beyond the circle of firelight, but they were absolute black, impenetrable. Half a year ago he'd have been terrified, sitting in the Pictish wilderness like this, knowing that those shadows might well be thick with Pictish warriors waiting for a chance to lop off his head to decorate the walls of their huts. Now, he had a completely different view of the Picts. And be-sides, there were none around but Kral, it seemed. "He helped us when we needed it. Are we to turn away when he needs us?"

"Some would."

"True enough. Not you—you sitting here in the cold is proof of that."

She pressed her shoulder against his—on the other side of many layers of fabric, at any rate—and tossed him a smile that felt like a blessing. "Does it mean we're stupid?" she asked.

He laughed. "Gullible, perhaps. Shortsighted. But if I was stupid"—he ticked his head to where Alanya and Kral lay, on the other side of the fire, at least two feet separating their slumbering forms—"I would be over there somewhere, instead of sitting with you."

She was silent for a bit, as if considering his words. He began to wonder if she had fallen asleep. Finally, she spoke again. "You know what? I believe you are right about that, Donial. Perhaps we're not stupid after all."

"Perhaps not," Donial said, pleased that the conversation was not over yet. He had wanted to guide it to a certain destination, but had been unable to find an easy way to do so. Instead, he just decided to say it. "Tarawa, that home, in Tarantia—I would love to take you there. To show you my city. Introduce you to my friends."

"Are you sure?" she asked, sounding surprised that he had brought it up.

"Of course," he said. "When this is all over, I don't want to lose you. Anyway, where else would you go?"

He felt her shrug through the fabric. "I haven't made any plans," she said. "I suppose there are worse places than Tarantia." She laughed lightly. "And worse people to be there with."

"We're in one of them right now," Donial said. "And I guarantee you, Tarantia is not nearly this cold."

"Then I'm for it," Tarawa replied. "And the sooner we get there, the more I'll like it."

19

DEMONSTRATING THEIR UNEXPECTED flexibility, the Picts staged their next major assault on Tanasul well after darkness had fallen. The fighting had continued throughout the day, but around dusk they had fallen back, taking to the cover of the trees. Some of the soldiers had cheered, but Sharzen, functioning as acting governor of the settlement, had done his best to persuade them that it was only a temporary thing, that the Picts had certainly not given up. He had proclaimed himself acting governor, however, and there were others in the town who disputed his claim. One of those, an army captain named Sulish, sounded off after listening to Sharzen's warning.

"Nonsense!" the man shouted. "They've realized that they cannot breach our defenses. Our soldiers are too skilled, our walls too solid, and the aid we've received from our neighbors has convinced them that we are not the easy target they expected. You cannot expect savages like them to continue to work toward a common goal when it is not easily met."

Sharzen spun around to see who contradicted him. He was not surprised to find that it was Sulish, who had been eyeing him suspiciously since he had arrived in the settlement. "Obviously you know little of the Picts," he countered. "They may be heartless savages, but they are nothing if not tenacious."

"And I tell you they are a cowardly lot and easily frightened off."

Sharzen shook his head sadly. "Have you ever met a Pict?" he asked. "I see by your armor that you are a soldier, but I am forced to wonder if you've fought the Picts, or you would know better."

"I grant you," Sulish said, "that one-on-one, they are formidable adversaries. But as a group, I think—"

"You are mistaken," Sharzen insisted, cutting the other man off. "You had all better keep watch on those trees!" he called to the soldiers on the wall. "Because they will be back. You can count on that."

Sulish had grumbled, but the guards had remained alert. Even so, by the time the attack came, many of them had been weary, distracted. Once again, the Picts dispensed with their usual battle cries. No one knew of their presence, it seemed, until their arrows felled the first soldiers.

The alarm was sounded. Sharzen, still inhabiting Pulliam's old office, heedless of the bloody streaks on the floor, heaved a great sigh and dragged on his mail shirt, cuirass, and helm. He slid his arm inside the straps of a heavy shield and took up a short sword. So equipped, he stepped outside to see what the situation was.

At the walls, soldiers were fighting and dying, and not just from arrows. The Picts must have been building ladders, for the battlements swarmed with them. They emerged from the night's shadows like ghosts, their body paint hiding them until they announced themselves with blood and iron.

Sharzen saw Sulish, running toward the wall. The soldier caught his eye for a moment but said nothing. That was fine with Sharzen. He knew who had been right, and so did the soldiers. Having accomplished that, he set about trying to find someplace safe to wait out the battle. There was always Pulliam's office, but many seemed aware of how much time he had been spending there. If he stayed in the same place all the time, he might be accused of cowardice. But if he moved around, there would be times when no one would know where to find him.

He headed deeper into Tanasul, where the streets were clogged with refugees from Koronaka and other, smaller settlements. They huddled against walls, some trying to sleep. In the torchlight, women, children, and the infirm stared up at him with the haunted eyes of the displaced. From here, the sounds of combat came to them, echoing horribly off the buildings, made worse, possibly, by the fact that they could not tell who lived and who died. People from Koronaka who recognized him tried to speak to him, but Sharzen pushed rapidly through the throng, kneeing the seated or squatting out of his way.

But his search was for naught. Everywhere he went, more refugees blocked his way. If he escaped the crowds, then he found himself back at the walls. The Picts had seemingly attacked simultaneously on every side. Sharzen found himself jostled by armored soldiers heading for the thick of it. "Come, man," one said, grabbing Sharzen's arm as he tried to hurry by. "We need all hands at the wall."

Sharzen tried to pull away, but then another soldier bumped into them. Neither of them was from Koronaka, and they did not recognize him, seeing only an armed and able man before them. "I am not a . . ." he began. But the other men moved on, not listening to his protests. Still, a seemingly constant stream followed in their wake. Sharzen glanced up at the nearest parapet, where Picts surged over the walls and engaged with the soldiers. Bodies dropped to the ground with disturbing regularity. *At least some of them belong to the savages,* Sharzen thought.

This did not bode well for his attempt at secure solitude, however. He now realized that staying in Pulliam's office might have been the best choice after all. Getting back there would be difficult.

Staying alive on that wall would be difficult, too, though. He made his decision, and started back the way he had come. The same crowded streets met him, and this time he could not ignore the shouts of some of the women. "Give us arms, Sharzen, and let us join our men on the wall!" one called.

"You may yet be called upon," he told her. "For now, stay with the children and the old ones. They need your comfort. The Picts are being routed," he added as he pressed on. It might have been a lie, of course—he had no way to tell what the status of the battle was. But he kept repeating it as he went, trying to bring some solace to those who waited for word. "We're whipping them!" he cried. "Even now the Picts realize their mistake in attacking us here!"

He knew he sounded like Sulish now, bringing false hope where there was none of the real kind to be had. But he addressed civilians, not soldiers. They seemed cheered by what he reported and made no move to impede his progress.

A short while later, he had reached the open square that Pulliam's office faced onto. The door to the office was open, firelight flickered inside. He could not remember if he had closed the door or not, and he assumed that he would not have extinguished the lanterns before he left it. Even so, he kept his sword ready and listened closely before entering.

The place seemed empty. Sharzen breathed a sigh of relief and was about to sheathe his blade when a figure parted from the shadows at the back of the room. It was an old man, a Pict. His hair was as much silver as black, and there were bird feathers entwined in it. He wore a ragged fur cloak fastened at the collar with a copper chain. Beneath it, his shoulder had been crudely bandaged. At his waist were a girdle and a loincloth. Leather sandals were strapped around his ankles. In his hand he carried a war axe, its head chipped from stone but with an edge that gleamed in the fire. He stared at Sharzen through narrow, angry eyes.

"Where is the crown?" the old man rasped in accented Aquilonian.

"What crown?" Sharzen replied, not sure he had understood the man correctly. But now he noticed that the man had apparently been searching for something. A massive wooden chest in which Pulliam had kept some of his personal things had been emptied haphazardly onto the floor. "Think you that there is a king here in Tanasul?"

"No crown of any Aquilonian king means aught to me," the Pict said. "The crown I seek belongs to the Picts, by right and by history. It was stolen from the Bear Clan, and we would have it back."

The Bear Clan! That was the bunch Lupinius had destroyed. Sharzen searched his memory, but could not recall anything about a crown, though. "You are mistaken," he said. "We have no such crown here."

"You can think about your answer for a few more seconds," the Pict said. "But then you will die, and it will be too late to change your story."

Sharzen dropped to a fighter's crouch, knees slightly bent to give himself better mobility. He raised sword and shield toward the half-naked savage, who now approached, swinging the big axe as if it weighed nothing. Even as he prepared himself to do battle, Sharzen could not ignore the irony that his own effort to find some other sanctuary had enabled this man to catch him unawares in the one place he really believed he was safe. . . .

USAM HAD CLIMBED one of the ladders along with a steady river of warriors. At the top, soldiers had tried to block their approach. But the Picts battled fiercely, and by the time Usam reached the parapet, it had been cleared of soldiers. Picts dropped from here to the ground and spread out to harass the Aquilonians. Usam followed suit, though the landing was hard on his old legs. A pair of soldiers had thought to capitalize on his first staggered steps, but he had shown them he was not slowed by a little pain. He'd screeched out a war cry and plowed into them with axe flying.

Once clear of the initial fight, he had worked his way quickly into the town, away from the walls. A big square led to a large, log building with a massive stone chimney. The structure looked important, particularly the way it commanded the square, so Usam set out for it first. The crown, if it was here, would most likely be kept in a place of honor, he reasoned. This place looked like the most prestigious building that he could see from here, so it was a start.

The building seemed empty when he went in. Lamps were lit, and the front door was open, so he assumed that whoever had been inside had rushed out when the attack came. That was fine with him—it gave him a chance to look around without having to kill more of the enemy first.

What he found seemed to be a public space, with long tables for eating and drinking. But beyond that was a smaller, enclosed space such as the fort's chief or commander might use as his headquarters. This was just what Usam had been hoping to find. He ransacked every space that might be big enough to hide the Teeth of the Ice Bear and had been about to go deeper into the building's interior when he'd heard the scuff of a boot on the outer steps. He stepped into black shadows at the back of the room, held his breath, and waited. Just one man entered. He was armed, but looked soft, bloated. Usam stepped out to face him.

Now that the man denied knowing anything about the crown, Usam prepared to split his skull. If the man was lying, he would speak up, or die. Either result would satisfy the Pict.

He could tell by the trembling of the man's arms when he lifted sword and shield that his foe was no warrior. Usam swung his axe in a slow circle, at his side, then over his head, as he approached. The Aquilonian's eyes grew wider, and he tried to ready himself for the first blow, but Usam kept varying the angle of the swing. Keeping his opponent guessing. The other man's lip quivered, and Usam wondered if he was going to beg for mercy. He hesitated a second, just in case the Aquilonian had decided to tell him where the crown was after all.

But the man simply closed his mouth again, as if

aware how it made him look. Tired of waiting, Usam charged.

OUTSIDE, A FEROCIOUS wind howled, loud as the souls of every wolf who had ever died, joining their voices. Conor sat inside his home with a fire crackling and a mug of ale close at hand. He had hung furs against the walls to provide one more barrier against the cold. Smoke blew back down the stone chimney from time to time, but he was warm and dry, and both things counted, on this strangest of Cimmerian autumn days, more than most.

The wind was so violent that he almost didn't hear the hammering on his door. Or to be more precise, he heard it, but didn't think it was anything more than something blown up against the door or an outside wall. He was not expecting anyone, and only the worst kind of imbecile would be about on a day like this one. It was only when the knocking turned into a determined pounding that he realized someone was outside. Reluctantly, Conor opened the door to admit whoever it was.

Snow blew into the hut when he tugged open the plank door. Two figures stood there, shadows against the field of white. The taller of them ducked his head to pass through Conor's doorway. Conor recognized the blunt features, the squarish head, the black hair hacked chin length with a knife. Roak Treefeller. Biggest man in Taern, with arms as massive as Conor's thighs. Behind him came Morne, more compact but with shoulders wider than an axe handle's length, a scar as big across as two of Conor's fingers running from chin to brow, and a perpetually angry expression because of it. He stepped back to admit them.

"What brings you out in this storm?" he asked.

"We wouldn't be out if it was not important," Roak assured him.

"It's Grimnir," Morne added.

"I've heard the name," Conor said. "A Vanirman, is he?"

"Vanir," Morne said with a nod. "But no mere man. A sorcerer of the worst kind."

"We believe him to be responsible for this weather," Roak said. "As a cover for an assault on Cimmeria. And a Cimmerian men call Wolf-Eye is leading a counterattack. Warriors from every village are joining Wolf-Eye's effort. We have rounded up Taern's best, and we leave today. Will you join us?"

Conor thought for a moment. He had only heard rumors of this Grimnir, and they all indicated that he was a great threat to every Cimmerian. But he had not heard of Wolf-Eye at all. It would no doubt be a dangerous campaign, not to mention cold and unpleasant.

Besides, if the rest of Taern's warriors left the village, who would be left to protect it from other threats? Who would be left to make love to its women? No, better that someone stay behind. And that someone would be he.

"I cannot join you," he said. "This Wolf-Eye is no one to me. My place is here in Taern, making sure no evil befalls our own people."

Roak and Morne locked eyes, and Morne's big shoulders moved in a faint shrug. "You would let your betters die protecting your homeland?" Roak asked.

"I told you it was pointless to ask him," Morne said.

"It is my homeland I'm thinking of," Conor said. "My home is Taern. I would not abandon it in a time of need."

Roak shook his great head slowly and started for the door. Morne fixed Conor with a look that, on his ruined face, was as fearsome as the visage of a horrific demon. "This will not be forgotten, Conor," he said. "Upon our return, there will come a reckoning."

"I wish you safe journeys," Conor said, crossing to close the door behind them. *And may your scarred, ugly head be ripped from your body and left to rot in the snow,* he thought but did not add. When the two were gone and the door closed, Conor went back to the fire and tossed another split log onto it. He would wait at least one day after they had left, maybe two, he decided. Then he would start to spread the word to the village's women that he had stayed behind to take care of them.

No matter what their needs might be.

20

THE BLACK RIVER'S source was a spring in the foothills, just across the border with Cimmeria. The spring fed a lake in a mountain meadow, and from the lake, water flowed into the channel that, many miles downstream where additional creeks and snowmelt fed into it, became the raging river they had navigated in Kral's canoe all this way. The lake was a deep indigo color, frozen at the edges, and around it the meadow was carpeted in white. There seemed to be no smell at all, or if there was, Alanya's nose had been frozen, and she could not detect it.

They all stepped from the canoe onto solid ice and dragged it to the shore, where Kral made it fast to a leafless tree. "We may need it again, when we have the rest of the teeth," he pointed out. "Best to know it will be here when we come back for it."

Alanya couldn't argue with that. She had not given much thought to getting back out of Cimmeria once the quest was over—if it even turned out that Conor had the missing teeth in his possession. It was just as possible that he had sold them, and they would be off again to some other part of the world.

But whenever it was all over, the hard decisions would come. Go back to Tarantia to run Father's business affairs, with Donial? Could the two of them ever agree on how to run a business? And what about Kral, who would take the crown back to its cave beneath the Bear Clan's home? And Tarawa—would she go to Aquilonia with them? She seemed to like Donial, and he was clearly smitten with her, so possibly.

On the way up the river, she could tell that Kral longed to be home again. Even though there was little left of his clan, he could join another clan or stay on at the Bear Clan village to help protect the Teeth of the Ice Bear. He had been worried about the emptiness of the land, the fact that all of the Picts seemed to have gone off someplace. Finally, as they worked farther north, they had seen the smoke from many fires, on the Aquilonian side of the Black. Kral had seemed heartened by the sight. "There they are," he had said, relief evident in the glow on his face. "Making war against the settlements is my guess. Mang meant to unite the clans against them, to regain the Teeth, and it looks as if he did so."

"Should we go to them?" Alanya had asked, worried

about the scale of the battle. "Tell them that the Teeth is not in the settlements at all?" She had been told that Conan was sending an army to help the settlers, and when it arrived, she feared the Picts would be destroyed completely. She was surprised that her loyalties had shifted toward the Picts in this case, but when she reflected on it, decided that what she truly longed for was peace. Neither side should be crushed under the other's heel, and both should learn to get along peacefully. Her father had given his life for the cause of peace between Pict and Aquilonian. Perhaps, she thought, there was a way that she could continue that legacy.

"We haven't time," Kral had replied. "If I could tell them that I have the Teeth, perhaps the war could be called off. But I cannot tell them that until the crown is made whole again. What if it turns out that your uncle sold the teeth before he even took the crown to Tarantia? They may still be in the Westermarck, for all we can say."

A number of arguments came to Alanya's mind, tripping over themselves before she could give words to them. Finally, she didn't bother. Kral had made up his mind. He was satisfied that the fires indicated the location of the Pictish clans and would not take time out of their journey to go to them with only a partial crown.

Instead, they had continued paddling the canoe upriver, against the stream. Alanya had comforted herself with a glance into her magic mirror, summoning the image of Invictus, her father. The last time he had looked into the mirror, it seemed, was when he had presented it to her, telling her that it was a special object she must always take care of. He had patted down his black hair, then moved closer to it, pulling up his eyelid. His mouth moved, and though she couldn't hear it, she remembered that he had said, "Something in my eye." Then he had touched his eyeball with his finger, apparently retrieving a trespassing eyelash. He'd handed the mirror back to Alanya then. She watched his motions in the mirror a couple of times, vowing to the image there that when this was over, she would do what she could to further the cause of peace, in his name.

Standing by the shore of the lake, she noticed that Tarawa shivered more than the others, even though she also wore the most. "Are you all right?" she asked the Kushite girl.

"Just . . . c-c-cold . . ." Tarawa stammered. "I . . . I had heard that Cimmerians were a h-hardy sort, but . . ."

"They are that," Donial answered. "Conor, the man we seek, is this tall." He held his hands up over his head, almost to their full length. Then he moved them out to his sides. "And this wide. He probably never feels the cold."

"He's still human," Alanya said, laughing. "He is no doubt more accustomed to it than you, Tarawa. But I'm sure he feels it."

"Perhaps," Donial said. "But I fail to understand how anyone who *can* feel cold would willingly return to such a place."

"It's his home," Kral suggested. "Everyone feels a special fondness for home, I believe, however wretched the place really is."

"I suppose," Tarawa said. She flapped at her arms with her hands and stomped her feet against the chill. "I have no desire to return to Dugalla, though I'd rather be there than here."

"We'll try to make this as fast as we can," Kral said. "And then depart for warmer climes, if any such still exist."

Even at the best of times, Alanya knew, Cimmeria was a cold and forbidding land, seldom visited by outsiders. But Elonius, the one surviving member of Gorian's mercenary crew, had been there, and claimed to know where the village of Taern was. He had drawn them a rough map, indicating that it was not far at all from this point, just a little to the south and east. He had indicated a few landmarks on it as well, the first of which was a peak shaped like a hunched-over woman. Looking in that general direction, they saw the peak, and it did resemble his description. Heartened by this discovery, they gathered their things from the bottom of the canoe, fixed them to their bodies, and started off on foot. Each step, Alanya prayed, would bring them closer to finishing this for good and all.

SHARZEN DUCKED UNDER the Pict's first blow and threw his shield up to deflect it. The axe glanced off the shield, but still Sharzen could feel its power in his shoulders and chest. He stabbed with the short sword, but the Pict danced away from the thrust. Sharzen backed him up with another couple of stabs, trying to take the measure of his opponent as he did.

The Pict was older than he, but strong, rangy. Light on his feet. He wielded the war axe like it weighed nothing. Scars crisscrossing his torso indicated that he'd been in battle many times before and survived. This would not, the governor knew, be an easy win.

But he was a survivor as well, and it would take more than one old Pict to bring him down. The Pict charged again, bringing his axe up in a swinging motion from lower right to upper left. If it had connected, the blow would have split Sharzen open, groin to shoulder. Sharzen sidestepped it. It was on the wrong side to block with his shield, but he kept his blade up and the axe's handle grazed it. He tried to follow up by slicing at the Pict's axe hand, but the old one yanked it out of the way, and the sword found only air.

He lashed out again toward the Pict's belly. The Pict dropped the head of his axe, parrying the thrust. Sharzen tried again, but his foe stepped away from the attack and reached out for Pulliam's chair, close beside him. Scooping it up in his left hand, he hurled the thing at Sharzen. Sharzen batted it out of the way but the Pict used the moment to come forward again, axe arcing toward him. Sharzen got his shield up just in time to block it.

But the axe did not bounce off the shield, this time. Instead, it plowed through the steel-and-leather construction, carving into Sharzen's upper left arm as it did. Sharzen let out a yelp of pain as he was driven to one knee. With the point of his sword, he held the Pict at bay long enough to force his left leg to straighten beneath him.

He stepped back, gaze locked on the Pict's eyes, waiting for the man's next attack. A table nudged the backs of his legs. He tried to recall the layout of Pulliam's office, but the Pict had moved things around in his search. Moving to his right, he felt with the backs of his thighs for the table's corner. His left arm throbbed; blood spilled down it, making the straps that held the wrecked shield on slippery.

Throwing the chair had been clever. A similar idea occurred to Sharzen. The shield was nearly useless for its original purpose. He shook it down his arm, letting it fall, then catching the second strap in his left fist. As the Pict circled toward him, Sharzen roared with pain and hurled the shield.

The Pict raised his axe and deflected the shield, sending it clanging against a wall. But even as he did, Sharzen was on the move. He threw himself to his knees, sliding along the floor, sword point out. The Pict tried to swing his axe from its raised position to intersect Sharzen's charge, but it sailed harmlessly over the Aquilonian's head. The sword point found the flesh of the Pict's thigh, dug in. Sharzen gave it a last push, then a twist before he wrenched it free and scuttled backward. The Pict's axe slammed into the floor where he had just been.

The Pict grimaced in pain, and blood ran from his thigh wound, splashing onto the floor. Slower on his feet than before, the Pict snarled and advanced again. Sharzen drew a dagger from his belt for his left hand. Teeth clenched, obviously fighting to ignore the agony,

the Pict limped forward with his axe raised. Sharzen
held both blades close together, waiting for the attack to
come. His left arm burned with pain, and he knew he
was losing too much blood to keep up the battle for
long. The time had come to end it.

When the Pict was off balance, limping toward him,
Sharzen struck.

USAM BIT BACK the pain in his thigh. The Aquilonian had surprised him with that move. He had never expected an opponent to willingly throw himself to the
floor. But the move had paid off, drawing blood and
slowing Usam down. Bad enough that his legs were still
aching from the long drop earlier, but now he thought
that his right would give out at any moment. His shoulder still throbbed from the earlier arrow wound, too.

His weight was on his weakened right leg when the
Aquilonian charged, his short sword and needlelike
dagger both flicking toward him. Usam threw his weight
back, onto his stronger left, and swept the axe up before
him, creating a barrier of wood and stone that blocked
both blades. The Aquilonian expelled his breath rapidly,
then muttered an oath that Usam couldn't understand.
Usam could see that the man was weakening because of
the blood running down his arm. The question was,
which of them would outlast the other? He also knew
that if either man managed to land another blow, that
would likely decide the conflict.

Steeling himself against the torment he knew was

coming, he threw his weight forward again, catching himself on his right leg. It nearly buckled beneath him, but held. At the same time he swung the axe in an arc over his right shoulder, bringing it down with all the strength he could command. The Aquilonian, back against a wall with nowhere to move, raised both his blades in an attempt to block the axe's descent.

The weight of his axe shattered the longer blade, and drove the dagger from the Aquilonian's weakened grasp. The man shouted a wordless cry and dove to the side. He hit on his right shoulder, rolled to his feet, and struck at Usam as the Pict was hoisting his axe again. This time, the man threw his arms around Usam and was able to drive the broken blade into Usam's side, behind the ribs. Usam screamed and broke the Aquilonian's grip. The man staggered back, into the wall again. Blinking sweat from his eyes, Usam rushed at his enemy. The man kicked the chair—the same one Usam had used before—into Usam's path. It tangled his legs, and Usam lost his balance. He flailed out, almost losing the axe, and crashed to the floor before the Aquilonian.

The other man still held his broken sword, its four inches of remaining blade slick with Usam's blood. He stabbed down at the fallen Pict. Usam writhed away from the blow and with his free hand caught the Aquilonian's ankle. He tugged, hard. The Aquilonian fought for balance, but his foot found a patch of blood on the floor and slipped out from under him. He collapsed to the floor, landing on his back, wincing in pain. Usam released his axe and threw his arm across his foe's chest, pressing him down. The Aquilonian tried to bring his broken sword into play, but Usam grabbed the man's hand with both of his.

The man struggled to get his sword hand free. Usam had the advantage of position, and in spite of his wounds was able to bring his weight to bear. He muscled the Aquilonian's hand around and got the blade fragment pressed against the man's collarbone. Wedged it there with his own hands, and let his weight push down on it. The Aquilonian hissed between clenched teeth, his eyes wide. He smacked ineffectively at Usam with his other hand.

"Know you where the crown is?" Usam asked him. "This is your last chance to save yourself."

The man's head twitched from side to side. He kept pressing back with the knife, hitting Usam's shoulder with his other hand. He tried to writhe under the Pict's bulk, to kick out with his legs. His wounds had sapped his strength, however. "I know nothing about any crown," he managed to gasp.

Hearing this, Usam arched his back, pushed his shoulders up, pressing down with all his weight on the blade fragment. It sliced into the man's neck, cutting down toward his throat. Usam felt hot blood splash his face and arms, and the Aquilonian, with a final burst of strength, jerked almost to a sitting position.

Just as quickly, though, the life flowed from him, and he sank back down. Usam held the hand with the sword hilt in it, sawing with the broken blade, until the Aquilonian was definitely gone. Finally, he released it, slumping over the body and breathing heavily for a few minutes. When he felt ready, he pushed himself to his feet, swayed, staggered, nearly fell again. He was weak, badly injured. He had held out longer than his opponent, but not by much.

The crown was still out there. If this Aquilonian did not know where, then some other one would. Usam would kill as many as he could with his own hands until he found it. His people, meanwhile, would kill the rest, put the torch to their settlements, search every cranny.

The storm outside was all the evidence Usam needed that time was growing short. The Ice Bear neared. Only the crown would turn the beast away.

On unsteady legs, Usam left the building, looking for more Aquilonians to kill.

21

CIMMERIA WAS NEARLY as empty as the Pictish lands, it seemed. Kral wondered for a moment if the Cimmerians had gone south to give aid to one side or the other in the conflict raging along the border. But that was a foolish thought, he decided immediately. The Cimmerians had no love for either side, or for any people but their own. Nothing could tempt them to throw in with either of those camps, he knew.

Still, it struck him as odd that they saw no riders, no one out hunting or chopping wood. On the way to Taern they passed a small village, a scattering of huts built around a larger lodge building. Smoke wafted up from a few fires, but looking down from the hillside Kral could see no men at all, just a few children wrestling and two women cooking something. There might have been others inside the huts—almost certainly there were. But just as certainly, the village was much emptier than usual. He had been worried about passing this close to a village, but it was obvious that there were no guards about, no warriors who would make them sorry they had happened across it.

Even so, they did not tarry, but kept on their way. Taern, according to the map Elonius had given them, was close by. The next village, just a few hills away. Kral noted with some pleasure that, like the Picts, the Cimmerians chose not to live right on top of one another, but spaced their villages out, and their homes within those villages.

Alanya and Donial had little problem keeping up, even through deep snow and punishing winds. Tarawa was slower, and needed help more often. Before this trip, she admitted, she had never seen snow. She had heard tales about it and always thought it sounded pleasant, white and fluffy, like clouds fallen gently to earth. Now she had learned that it was cold and wet, and slogging through it was exhausting. She tried not to complain, and whenever Kral checked on her she pasted a brave smile to her face, but he could see that it was taking a lot out of her.

With any luck, once they reached Taern they would get the missing teeth back from Conor, then she and the others could rest there for a few days while Kral hurried the crown back to its cave.

When they finally saw Taern ahead, on their second afternoon in the country, the sun had already slipped behind glowering clouds. It was not full dark yet, but the days were not bright to begin with. The skies were as gray as lead, and when the sun did peek through the gloom its light was thin and brought little warmth. A frigid wind blew from the north, gaining in intensity as the sun lowered.

They decided that stealth was neither necessary nor possible, so they simply walked into the town. A couple of children, scampering around on the frozen earth, saw them, stopped, and ran for the nearest hut. A moment later, a woman came out, bent and gray, walking with the aid of a gnarled stick.

"If you've come to steal from us, you're too late," she said, breaking into a cackling laugh. "We've precious little left to take."

Kral could see at a glance that she was right. Woodpiles were low. No meat hung alongside the lodge building, nor was there any roasting over the small fires. The children were bundled in furs that looked old, handed down from generation to generation.

"We want nothing from you," Kral answered. Many Picts from his part of the wilderness spoke at least rudimentary Cimmerian, as there was uneasy trade across the border from time to time. "If this is Taern, we seek one of your men."

"If it's an old one, you might be in luck," she said, still laughing. "Or a lazy one—we've a few of those left."

"His name is Conor," Kral said. "He was in Aquilonia recently."

The woman's eyes narrowed, her smile vanishing.

"Lazy, then," she said. She pointed downslope with her stick at a hut with thick smoke roiling from a chimney. "Him, you can have. You'll find him there."

Kral thanked her and translated the message for the others. "Lazy sounds right," Donial said, with a chuckle.

"At least he has a fire going," Tarawa observed. "I would kill to sit inside next to a fire."

"No killing," Kral warned. "At least until after I have my teeth." Realizing what he had said, he put his fingers in his mouth, as if counting. "I mean, the crown's teeth," he added.

Tarawa laughed in spite of her obvious discomfort. Shivering, she started down the slope toward Conor's hut, and the others joined the march. In a few moments, they stood outside his door. Kral rapped on the frozen planks. In return, they heard a muffled shout. Kral didn't understand it, but it did not sound welcoming.

"Let me," Donial said. He shoved impatiently past Kral and leaned on the door, forcing it open. "Conor, we know you're in here!" he called.

When Donial had the door wide, Kral could see Conor inside, grabbing at a sword that sat, sheathed and attached to a curled belt, on a nearby table. He wore a woolen vest and leather breeches, but his huge arms and feet were bare.

"You!" he shouted. "What do you want? I did your job for you!"

"Part of it," Donial acknowledged.

Conor rose from his chair, holding the belt and sword, still scabbarded. "I know not why you're here, but you had better go," he said. "This is my home, my village. With a word from me, you'd all be torn to shreds."

"That is not what the woman who told us where to find you said," Kral pointed out.

Conor scoffed. "She must be one I have not yet pleasured," he said.

"Maybe if you had started from the oldest and worked down," Tarawa said with a grin, "you'd have reached her first."

Conor puffed himself up to his full height, swelling his chest. He really was huge, Kral noted. He didn't want to have to fight the Cimmerian, but he would if it came to that. In the meantime, Conor was doing his best to frighten them off without resorting to actual violence. "I am serious," he said in a kind of low growl. "I have had my fill of you, and I did not invite you into my home. Now I'm telling you, get out before there's trouble."

"There's already trouble," Kral told him. "If you have something that is not yours."

Conor shrugged. "I have been a thief, among other things. What of it?"

"It's a specific thing we seek," Alanya said. She gave Tarawa a gentle nudge toward the fire and leaned against the edge of the table from which Conor had taken the sword. Legs crossed at the ankles, arms folded over her chest, her entire manner was relaxed, casual. "Give it to us and we'll gladly leave you alone."

"Because I'm sure the women of Taern resent the time we're taking up," Donial added. He tried to hide his smile by looking away from the Cimmerian.

"Some teeth," Kral put in. "From the Pictish crown. We believe you had your hands on them at some point. I need them back."

"What if I don't have them?" Conor demanded.

"Then you'll find them and get them back for me," Kral said. "Or you'll regret it for the rest of your extremely short life."

Now Conor laughed. "You threaten me?" he asked. "Remember who you address, boy."

"I address a bloated, half-drunk, frightened barbarian," Kral challenged. "Who may think he's the better of us, but who will quickly find out he's wrong if I do not get those teeth right now."

Conor moved faster than Kral had expected, whipping the big blade from its scabbard and throwing the belt to one side. "I'll not stand and listen to the likes of that from you," he said.

Kral dropped back a step, his hand going to his own sword. It was not a natural weapon for Picts, but he had come to recognize its usefulness and had become more than a little skilled with it. "You have no choice in the matter," he countered.

"I do if I split you from gullet to stern."

"Think you that you can defeat us all, Conor?" Donial asked. He had also filled his hand with steel. Kral saw Conor's gaze flit across the room, realizing as it did that Alanya and Tarawa had spaced themselves out around him. Each of them held a sword now.

"Four against one?" Conor said with a laugh. "And

you children? Go find a few more friends so the odds
will be more even."

"These odds are fine," Kral said. He was suddenly as
serious as death. "The teeth, Conor."

Conor's mood changed to reflect Kral's. Kral could
see the Cimmerian's fingers tighten on his grip. *So
it starts,* he thought. A close quarters battle in a small
space, with too many combatants for easy movement.
Someone would die in the next few minutes. He knew
they were all prepared for the possibility. His friends
had changed since he'd met them. He supposed he had,
too. Alanya and Donial had spent enough time in his
company that the veneer of civilization had fallen from
them. There had been a time when they would have insisted on a "fair" fight. Now they understood that when
people were going to die, it was always better to be on
the side that won the battle.

"It is not too late, Conor," he said. "What good are
the teeth to you? Why risk losing everything for them?"

Conor didn't answer. Not with words. Kral caught
the slight shift of his eyes that meant he was attacking,
and he brought his sword up just in time to block
Conor's first blow. But the broadsword was massive,
and Conor put all his strength behind it. Kral success-
fully deflected it, but the effort staggered him. He would
not be able to block many of those blows.

Conor's muscles tensed to attack again. His attention
was focused on Kral, however, and Donial—speedy Donial, Kral thought with pleasure—darted in as if from
nowhere. He didn't manage to sink his blade deep in the

Cimmerian's flesh, but grazed his right arm, drawing first blood. Conor clapped a hand over the wound, and it came away sticky. He eyed Donial. "So," he said, "this is how it's to be?"

"You said we had not evened the odds sufficiently," Alanya pointed out. "You can always call off the fight by turning over the teeth."

"What makes you think I even have them?" he asked.

"The Stygians who stole the crown never saw them," Alanya explained. "But we know you found the thief, spoke to him. He was the likeliest person to have removed them from the crown. And we know what you are like—if there was a way you could take advantage of us, you would."

Conor made a wounded face. "I am hurt," he said. "That you would think ill of me." Before he even finished his sentence, he lashed out at Donial, who had not backed far enough away to avoid the big sword. Tarawa interceded, though, her own blade snaking between them so that Conor's broadsword was knocked harmlessly to one side. Kral took advantage of the moment to strike with his, ripping the fabric of Conor's vest and carving a line up his chest. Blood beaded along the cut.

"I may have . . . underestimated . . . the four of you," Conor admitted. "You have fangs, after all."

Alanya held her sword out toward him with a steady hand. "Even if you do defeat us," she said, "you will have some wounds to explain to the women of Taern when next you see them. Wounds that you'll have to confess were dealt by 'children,' as you call us. Would it not be easier simply to let Kral have his teeth?"

Conor looked at each one in turn, his gaze finally coming to rest on Kral. Kral understood that the Cimmerian was measuring him up, knowing that, while he was outnumbered, it was the Pict who was the serious threat. Kral measured Conor at the same time. Bigger than he, heavier, greater reach. Much more experience, especially with a sword.

At the same time, he knew he could take the man. Conor didn't have the fire in his eyes, the look of a man who would do anything to win. His cheeks were soft, flabby, and circles under bloodshot eyes spoke of a man who didn't sleep well. Where his vest had come open, Kral saw that his belly was rounded. He was a muscular man who had stopped using those muscles, for the most part. Conor relied on his size and reputation to intimidate his opponents now, Kral speculated. And while the man was still a formidable warrior, he was no longer good enough to beat Kral.

This new certainty gave him confidence. He started to move again, just a step or two in one direction and then the other. Not enough room in here for real maneuvering, but he would be fine. He kept his gaze on Conor and could almost see the Cimmerian wither under its intensity.

Finally, Conor lowered his weapon. "I haven't been able to sell them anyway," he said. "They do me no good, and obviously have brought me nothing but trouble. You're welcome to them."

Before Kral could answer, a blast of wind rattled the

hut. The door shook as if a giant hand tried to tear it from its hinges. Conor looked up, startled. "Another storm," he said. "Sounds like a bad one."

"We have miles to cover yet," Donial said.

"Not in this weather," Conor answered. "From the sound of it, you won't make it beyond the village boundaries." He crossed to the door, heedless now of the weapons the others still held. When he opened it, a bitter wind blew in. Outside, all was white. Kral couldn't even see the nearest hut. "Ice storm," he said. "You'd all freeze to death in no time."

"But . . . we can't stay here," Tarawa said.

"There's nowhere else you can go," Conor replied, slamming the door against the weather. "You can't see five feet out there. Have you ever been in a Cimmerian ice storm, any of you?"

"No," Kral admitted. "We have not."

"You might make a quarter mile—blinded, but trudging into the wind. After that, the ice would cake on your flesh, burning it. Your joints would freeze up. You couldn't catch your breath. Before you were a half mile out, you would be stopped, crouching close to the ground for warmth, which you would not find. Your feet would freeze to the earth, then your hands. In the morning, or whenever the wind died, someone might find you, frozen in place, dead. They could snap your limbs off like dry twigs, crack your skin like frozen water."

"What is it to you?" Alanya asked. "A minute ago, you wanted to kill us anyway."

"In fair combat," Conor said. He went to his fire and

put on two more logs, poking the coals with the tip of his sword. In a moment, small blue flames licked at the first of the logs. "But now I've already told you I'll give you the accursed teeth you seek. I've nothing to fight you for, nor do you have reason to want me dead. I would not send you into that storm, knowing it would be the end of you."

"You would let us wait out the storm in your hut?" Tarawa asked. She looked astonished. Kral realized that he was as well. He guessed that Conor was simply being realistic—that having decided he couldn't beat them all, he might as well be hospitable so they didn't decide to kill him and just take the hut for themselves.

"It would not be my first choice," Conor admitted. "But it seems to be the only one." He reached into a rough wooden cupboard near the fire, brought out a heavy black pot and some dried meat. Handing a second pot to Kral, he said, "Get some snow in here that we can boil for water. And be quick about it, boy. I don't want to have to go outside looking for you."

22

CONOR SURPRISED THEM all, sharing elk meat with them and brewing a foul-smelling but hot concoction that warmed Kral's innards even as it turned his stomach. As the night wore on, Conor told stories of life in Cimmeria, other storms he had weathered, and his adventures in Aquilonia. In return, the others took turns telling their stories, detailing how Alanya and Kral had met, how they came to be in Tarantia and then Stygia with Donial, and how Tarawa had helped them retrieve the crown from her master.

Finally, as Kral was beginning to grow drowsy, Conor dug into a wooden box near the pallet he slept on and retrieved the missing teeth. He handed them over with only momentary hesitation. Once Kral had them in his hands, he fished the crown from its sack and went to work restoring the teeth to their rightful positions. It was late; Donial and Tarawa were already asleep, and Alanya was beginning to doze. Even Conor turned away after giving Kral the teeth and stretched out on his pallet.

Outside, ice driven by screaming winds pounded the hut like a thousand fists. Conor's meal, the furs on the walls, and the fire he kept carefully tended maintained a steady temperature inside, and Kral was warmer and more comfortable than he had been since they'd left Stygia. He was weary, and the idea of sleep appealed to him. But getting the teeth back had boosted his energy. He sat in Conor's chair and worked the teeth into place, twisting the fine copper wire, originally crafted so many generations ago, around the roots to hold them.

As he worked, he felt the weight of history, of responsibility, pressing down on him. Retrieving the crown from Shehkmi al Nasir had been an accomplishment, but tempered by the fact that some of the teeth were missing. Now that he finally had them all, he knew the moment of decision was upon him.

Mang waited back at the Bear Clan village to take over as Guardian of the Teeth, his proper role as village elder. The best thing Kral could do would be to leave now—or in the morning at the latest—and rush the crown back to the cave. He didn't know how long the storm would continue, and from the sound of it, Conor had not exaggerated its intensity. But he could not stay penned up here in Cimmeria while some unknown disaster loomed over all the Pictish people.

Alanya would not want to go back into the Pictish

wilderness, though. Despite having shed the delicate skin of civilization, her rightful place was in Tarantia. To fulfill his obligation to his people meant giving her up, probably forever. With so few members of the Bear Clan left, he would have to stay at the village to protect the Guardian's cave once the crown was back.

The thought of it made him cringe inwardly. He had grown used to being with her. They had never so much as shared a kiss, but he felt as if letting her go would mean losing the best friend he'd ever had—and maybe more. Maybe the woman who could make him happy for the rest of his life. Would he ever find her like again? She was so different from the Pictish girls he had known, not just physically, but in every way. He supposed that some of what he valued in her, ironically, came about because of her civilized upbringing.

Kral held the finished crown in his hands, feeling an odd vibration from it, a kind of *thrum* of untapped power. As he did, he looked at his friends, sleeping in the glow of Conor's fire. Each of them would gladly have sacrificed everything for his quest—as Mikelo had. He was pleased that the others had not been asked to give their lives. Now, it seemed, only one danger remained— the weather. And if he left now, while they slept, then they would not have to face that one. Conor could help them back to Aquilonia when the storm had passed.

He knew that Conor had warned them against try- ing to travel during the storm. But perhaps he had sim- ply been trying to spare the civilized ones—and Tarawa, accustomed only to hot climates. A Pict could navigate any kind of weather, Kral believed. With another quick glance around to make sure the others were all sleeping, he went to the door and opened it, just a crack, to take a look at this supposedly impassable storm.

And when he did, he saw three hooded Stygians looking back at him.

THE BATTLE FOR Tanasul wasn't won yet, but Klea was sure the tide had turned. She ran through the streets with her fellow warriors, brandishing a spear that had already been blooded numerous times and looking for more soldiers to use it on.

All Pictish women would fight if their homes were attacked, and most had no problem with hunting for meat and skinning what was caught. But few went on offensive missions like this one. Klea had found, though, that her time as the "Ghost of the Wall," mounting solitary attacks against Koronaka, had given her a taste for battle that could not be easily set aside. She felt more at ease with the warriors now than she did with the women who stayed behind, tending to fires, families, and food. They did not know the terrifying thrill of painting their faces and sneaking into the midst of their enemies, with only their own skills, stealth, and strong arms standing between themselves and certain death. They had never felt the power of the kill, knowing that the life of another human was theirs for the taking.

So she went over the wall with the other warriors, and already four soldiers had fallen before her tonight.

It was as if she could feel her own blood coursing through her veins, as if her senses were alive in a way they only were when she was in the thick of action. The soldiers had fallen back from this section of wall, giving it over to the Pictish hordes.

Her comrades thinned out as they worked their way deeper into Tanasul, branching out into different streets. Klea found herself on a quiet lane with three others. They had tried another street, but found it clogged with women and children, noncombatants, cringing in terror at the Pictish advance. Instead of wasting time with them, they had tried a few side streets, looking for the soldiers who had run back this way.

The whole town smelled of smoke and blood and the sweat of unwashed mobs afraid for their lives. Klea tried to breathe through her mouth as she hurried through it, longing for the clean air of the forest. An unbelievably cold wind whistled through the streets as if joining with the Pict warriors, and that wind was the only thing that kept Klea from choking on the stench surrounding her.

Suddenly seven soldiers erupted from an arched doorway, swords flashing in the moonlight. The nearest Pict went down immediately, fountaining blood from the neck. Another fell back, stabbed through the chest. Klea thrust her spear into the midst of the armored men. It grazed metal but did not pierce flesh. The Pict beside her swung a war club at the closest soldier. It connected with his helmet, and the man crumpled.

In just moments, Klea stood alone, facing three soldiers. Before her, a wounded Pict lay on the ground, clawing at the paving stones. He would live, she thought, if she could get him help. But the soldiers would as soon see both of them dead.

She weighed her chances. Three, and all of them wearing mail shirts and helmets, armed with short swords and a single halberd.

Her, in ragged skins with her spear, its edge dulled by use. A bone knife at her belt.

They were soldiers, though. Aquilonians, most likely, or some such who had thrown in with them. Civilized folk.

And Klea was Pict.

Shrieking a war cry, spear clutched in her fists, she charged.

A flashing web of steel. She felt her spear penetrate mail, felt pliant flesh and organs beneath it. Heard the cries of those she wounded. Smelled their fear, the fresh blood that spattered on her.

Barely felt, in her bloodlust, the cuts, the stabs. Steel opening her skin, her veins.

As the life ran out of her, as her soul prepared for its final journey, to the Mountains of the Dead, Klea knew that she died as a Pict and that her soul would not travel alone.

"CONOR!"

Kral knew he would only have time to call one name, so he chose the one likeliest to rouse everyone. He was standing in the doorway, holding the Teeth of the Ice Bear, and the three Stygians advanced upon him. He barely noticed that the snow and ice melted where their feet touched the ground. He could not close the door—some force seemed almost to have paralyzed him on the spot.

Behind him, commotion told him that the others were awake. "Crom's blood!" Conor swore. Tarawa added something in Kushite that Kral couldn't understand. He heard steel clearing scabbards, then the spell that held him in place broke.

"We would have the crown," one of the Stygians said. His voice was deep, sonorous, and Kral realized he could understand the words although he could not have said what language they were spoken in. The hooded men were interchangeable, as far as he was concerned—of similar size and coloration. They could have been the acolytes he had seen deliver the crown to al Nasir, with a new one added to replace the one the mage had killed, or three different ones of the same type.

Kral still held the crown in front of him, with both hands. From behind, he felt Conor nudge past him, then Tarawa and Donial. Alanya stopped at his side. Each of them held a sword.

"Think you that steel is a threat to us?" one of the acolytes asked.

"If you live, it can gut you," Conor answered. He charged them, swinging his huge broadsword with a stroke that would have sliced the head off a bull. But the frontmost Stygian waved his fingers at Conor and uttered a few incomprehensible syllables, and Conor stopped short. He screamed and dashed his weapon to the ground. His sword had become a red-and-black-striped serpent, which flicked its tongue at him and wriggled off across the ice.

"Again, we would have the crown," the acolyte repeated.

Kral's mind whirled. He could not let them have it. But so far the Stygians had only performed their magic against a weapon. He had seen what it could do to a person, in al Nasir's temple hideaway. If he did not give them the Teeth, then his friends would surely die—and he, as well. Then who would protect the crown from them?

No, he thought. No matter the price, he would not turn it over. If he went down, at least it would be holding a weapon, and with some Stygian blood on his hands. Having nothing better to do with the crown while he drew his sword, he lifted it and set it on his own head.

Scarcely had the sacred crown touched Kral's scalp when the world fell away beneath him, spinning, a whirlwind of color and sound and smell where moments before had only been fields of white, the Stygians, and his friends. He seemed to spin faster, ever faster, the colors blurring into solid black, then it was all gone, Cimmeria and Conor's hut and the ice, Alanya and Donial, Tarawa, everything that had been there had vanished, and Kral found himself in . . .

. . . where?

SMOOTH ROCK UNDER his feet, solid and unyielding. Kral took comfort from that. The feel of a stone floor was familiar, at least.

Nothing else was.

He seemed to be in a cavern, but one impossibly vast. He could see one wall, stretching toward what should have been sky. No stars shone there in the darkness, though, and from the shadows he could see what appeared to be the bottoms of stalactites, looking wet in the dim distance. The wall was also stone, but looked slick, viscous. All the colors of the rainbow were trapped within its layered surface. Kral turned, slowly, but the other walls were as far away as the ceiling. All was dark. He sniffed the air and found that it reminded him of the aftermath of lightning. The only sound was his own heavy breathing.

On an impulse, he reached up. The Teeth of the Ice Bear still rested on his head.

"Hello?" he asked. Then, louder. "Hello!"

They came into view gradually, as if a lantern were being turned toward them. Or else his eyes were just growing accustomed to the dark. But one minute he could see nothing, and the next, he could see men. Picts.

First two, then ten, then a thousand. Ten thousand. More, in numbers beyond counting.

They were ranked against the far, dark walls, where he knew his vision could not penetrate. They filled the cavern before him. They stood where he did—when he moved his hand, it passed through them. They milled about, their bodies without substance, walking through him as if he was not even there.

Ghosts, then.

"Where am I?" Kral demanded, even though he thought he already knew.

"Where do you think?" a voice asked.

He looked for the speaker, in the midst of all the others. And saw him. He stood in a line with four others, not far away, on a kind of dais. A golden glow fell on those five, although not on the rest. Of all the Picts Kral could see, only these five looked at him with anything like awareness, recognition.

The five—two women, three men—all wore cloaks of fur worked through with filaments of silver and gold, and decorated with multicolored feathers bigger than any ever worn by eagle or vulture, in Kral's experience.

"I think . . . I fear that I am dead," Kral said. "The Stygians have slain me."

One of the women smiled, as if Kral had told a joke. "Wrong," she said. "Not far off, but wrong nonetheless."

"Enough riddles, then," Kral said, anger bubbling up in him. "If I am not dead, then tell me where I am!"

"You are, as I believe you suspect, inside the Mountains of the Dead," one of the men told him. "But you are not yourself dead."

"Then why . . . ?" he began, confused. "And what gods are you?"

"No gods at all," the woman who had spoken before answered. "We are your ancestors, Kral. A thousand years after our deaths—or more—you came from our children and our children's children. That, and the fact that you wear the Teeth of the Ice Bear crown, are the reasons that we can talk to you. We know of your quest, and now you have succeeded in retrieving and making whole the sacred crown."

The man took up the narrative. "But we must warn you that time is short. The Ice Bear is on the move, and all Pictdom is in jeopardy."

"The Ice Bear?" Kral echoed.

"You have seen the storm that rages down from the north," the man said. "It shows no sign of lessening in power or severity as it moves south, out of Vanaheim and Cimmeria. This can only be the result of the Ice Bear's reawakening because the crown was taken from its rightful place."

"But . . . if it has already begun," Kral asked, "then can anything be done to stop it?"

"It can be stopped," the woman said. She had an expression of the utmost contentment on her face, as if there were no brewing crisis at all. "Here is what you must do. . . ."

AGAIN THE NAUSEATING spinning sensation, the vertiginous whirl of color and light. When his feet were back on solid ground, Kral felt a sudden sensation of cold and realized that, while he had been at the Mountains of the Dead—if in fact it had not just been a strange, waking dream—he had been briefly out of the elements.

But when his vision cleared, he realized he was right back where he had been, and no time at all had passed. The Stygians glared at him and his friends. The snake that had been Conor's broadsword was still in sight, slithering away. Alanya's arm brushed against his. Had he really been away?

"We would—"

"I know!" Kral interrupted. "You would have the crown. Well, I would not give it to you, so you will just have to do without."

The Stygian in front began to raise his hand toward Kral, as he had done toward Conor's sword. Kral knew that whatever he had in mind would not be good. He had only seconds, if that, to decide if he would follow the instructions given to him by his ancestors.

He knew, too, that Mang was the right person to take over as Guardian of the teeth. Mang was the village elder now. He deserved the role and was expecting it. But if Kral were to try to deliver the crown to the cave, it would likely never make it. He didn't have the magic to defeat these Stygians, and it looked as if steel alone would not do the job.

But Alanya! He would never see her again.

He looked at her. Her clear blue eyes, her golden hair reddened by henna, her creamy skin. More than anything, he wanted, at that moment, to draw her into his arms, to feel the warm bulk of her body against his, to taste her cherry lips.

"Kral . . . ?" she asked, surprised by his sudden, intense gaze.

"Alanya . . ." He couldn't finish the thought. Not for the first time, his grasp of the Aquilonian language failed him when it was most important to choose the right words.

But ultimately, there were no words that would help. He snatched the crown off his own head. Turned it over, so the jagged teeth faced down. As two of the Stygians broke into a run, trying to grab it while they could, and the other one finished whatever spell he planned to use, Kral jammed the crown back down on his head, upside down. The teeth gouged his flesh. Blood ran from the lacerations, streaking down his face, his neck.

And then darkness. . . .

23

ALANYA'S STOMACH LURCHED.

One moment, Kral was there, facing al Nasir's acolytes. The next, a strange sensation swept through her, but it was nothing she could define. Then everything seemed normal again, but after sharing a brief glance, Kral had reversed the crown on his head, ripping his own flesh in the process.

And then . . .

And then he was just gone. "Kral!" she shouted. She heard Donial and Tarawa both call him as well.

The Stygians stopped in their tracks, staring, snow and ice turning to liquid beneath their feet. One of them uttered something that sounded like a curse, except she realized she could no longer understand their words. Tarawa rushed them, her steel lashing out like sudden lightning. She drove it through the nearest one's heart, then wrenched it free and swung at the next. Alanya saw the third prepare to cast some kind of spell, but before she could even react, Donial was there with his own sword. Almost as one, he and Tarawa struck down the remaining two Stygians. Where their blood ran, the snow steamed.

Once they had fallen, an almost supernatural quiet descended. Three dead men melting the snow. Kral, disappeared.

Alanya felt a deep, powerful sense of loss. She seemed to know, somehow, that he was not coming back. A tear sprang to her eye, and she wiped it away, lest it freeze there.

"Where did he go?" Tarawa asked.

"You saw what we did," Donial reminded her.

"Accursed Stygian magic," Conor said, snarling at the dead acolytes. "Where have you sent him?"

Alanya put a restraining hand on the big Cimmerian. "It wasn't them," she said.

"How do you know? You can't trust a Stygian,"

"I just . . . I just do," Alanya replied. "I cannot tell you how, but I'm certain of it. Kral is where he needs to be."

"What does that mean?" Donial asked. "Where he needs to be?"

"Back at the . . . at that cave? Where the crown came from?" Tarawa guessed.

"I think so," Alanya said. "That's the only thing that make sense to me."

"What sense is that?" Conor wondered. "Sorcery most foul, I'd say."

"Sorcery?" Alanya echoed. "Perhaps. But it is what he wanted most."

Donial took Alanya's hand. "To leave you behind, sister? I do not think he wanted that."

"I doubt he had a choice," Alanya said. She appreciated her brother's thoughts and agreed that Kral would probably have wanted a different option—one that included her. Presumably that option had not presented itself, however, and he had done what was best for his people.

She would have expected nothing less.

Conor went back into his hut. Donial and Tarawa followed. Alanya stayed where she was a while longer, watching as the footprints where Kral had been standing were filled in by drifting snow.

When she got back inside, she was shivering, her teeth chattering uncontrollably. Conor had stoked the fire, and the flames roared, blasting warmth into the small space. Every place she looked reminded Alanya of Kral, even though they had only been here for a short time. The chair he'd sat in, the sack he'd carried the crown in. That reminded her of her own mirror, passed down from mother to daughter, and in which she could see the image of Kral whenever she needed to. She would not do it right now—the loss of him was too fresh, and seeing him would be far too painful. But later, she would, and even if it showed him in someplace where she could never reach him, at least she could gaze upon him. Maybe, in some way, he would know she was there.

The time she had spent with Kral had been the

strangest, most exciting, memorable period of her life. She could not say, at this moment, whether she would ever have another adventure like that. Part of her desperately hoped not—it had often been terrifying, and she'd been afraid on numerous occasions that they would never make it out alive.

She took up a mug of the stuff Conor had made for them, sipped from it, not even tasting. She felt the warmth fill her belly. Smiled at Donial, who sat close to Tarawa, clutching her dark hand in his pale one. Smiled, even, at Conor, who had caused them so much trouble and danger.

She didn't know why, but she was in a very forgiving mood.

ROAK TREEFELLER, MORNE, and the rest of the men from Taern stopped at the crest of a jagged ridge-line. Morne was the first one to notice what had changed, what had made them all halt at once. "It's the wind," Morne shouted. "Feel it!" He held his hand out as if to demonstrate.

Roak did the same, then extended his tongue as if to taste it. Warm. Sweet. "It's from the south," he said, surprised. "It's shifted."

"Right," Morne agreed. He fell silent then, tugging off his outer fur. The other men did the same. Roak, mystified, felt the wind again. It blew harder now, as hard as the north winds had, like air blasting from a huge fire. The harder it blew, the hotter it got. Ice melted from trees, dripping onto the ground, where it joined the snow that turned to water under the strange wind's influence. As they stood there on the ridge, the gray clouds parted, dissipated, as quickly as smoke on a breezy day. Roak could see the valley below, and it was obvious even from here that the same transformation took place there.

As suddenly as it had come up, the wind died. "Sorcery," Roak said uncomfortably.

"Aye," Morne agreed. "But not the worst kind, eh?"

Roak didn't like sorcery at all. But as he felt the warm air, saw the concentration of ice disappear, he could not disagree with Morne's conclusion,

Better this kind than the magic that had caused the ice storm in the first place. He didn't know if it meant that Grimnir was dead—or if the whole thing had been someone else's doing.

Perhaps he never would.

If Wolf-Eye still needed their help, the warriors of Taern would go to his side. But the going would be much easier, this way.

He knew that thanking Crom would be useless. The Cimmerian god would not have interfered in such a way.

But as they started down the other side of the hill, Roak issued silent thanks to whoever was behind it.

GESTIAN STOOD ON the ramparts of Tanasul with a half dozen of his best men around him, looking down into the settlement instead of out at the forest. Picts had been thronging the city, but now there were none to be seen. There were corpses everywhere. Blood filled the cracks between paving stones and collected in pools, drawing flies and other vermin. Tanasul would need major repairs and cleanup before it would be fit for human habitation again.

"They're gone," one of the soldiers said, interrupting his contemplation.

"They seem to be," Gestian agreed.

"But where? Why?"

"Who knows the minds of those savages?" Gestian replied. It wasn't much of an answer, but it was the best one he had. "Perhaps all they ever meant was to harass the settlements, to make us reconsider our presence here. As they did with the wall project, in Koronaka."

One of the other men snorted angrily. Gestian knew he'd had family in Koronaka—a wife and two children who had been with the party that was attacked on the way to Tanasul. None of them had survived. "Would that they'd have stayed and fought," he said bitterly. "Save me the trouble of chasing them into the woods to kill them."

"You'll never kill all the Picts," Gestian said. "King Conan is right. Better to make peace with them because they'll always be with us."

Even as he spoke the words, a lookout on the eastern wall cried out. "Aquilonian banners!" he shouted. "I can see the lion! And a lot of them!"

"There it is," Gestian said. "Reinforcements from the King. The Pictish scouts must have spotted them earlier, and that's why they drew back."

"Savages and cowards," the man who had lost his family insisted. "With any luck, the King's orders were to follow them into their own lands and wipe them off the face of the Earth."

Gestian shook his head, but remained silent. He knew such an order was most unlikely given Conan's professions of peace. He also knew, glancing down at the dead all around, that the Picts were no cowards. Savages, perhaps, for what that was worth. But he had taken part in the raid on the Bear Clan village that seemed to instigate all this trouble. He had seen the destruction that Lupinius and his Rangers had caused, and, in the heat of the battle, he and his fellow soldiers of Aquilonia had joined in. So he was not about to make judgments about the relative savagery of his own kind versus that of the Picts. They were the enemy, but they had fought well and bravely, and if it was the coming of the Aquilonian reinforcements that had chased them off, he was glad of it.

For his part, he would be happy never to cross weapons with the Picts again. The price of peace was high, but the cost of war ever so much higher.

With a shrug and a smile for his comrades, Gestian went to the ladder, to climb down and greet the Aquilonian troops.

THE DEATHS OF his acolytes woke Shehkmi al Nasir from a deep slumber with a sensation like needles piercing his temples. These magics were wearying, and grew more so with every passing year. He had hoped that, among other things, the mystical energies of the ancient crown would help restore his strength.

But when he tried to locate the crown once again, he could not. The smoke window that should have shown it failed him. It remained empty, a blank gray screen. He cursed, extinguished the fire, and tried again, with the same disappointing result.

Furious, he stormed around the room, inhaling the enchanted smoke and swearing at the ceiling. That crown should have been his! *Had been* his, for a distressingly brief time. With all the effort he had gone through to send acolytes after it—twice!—the fact that it was still not in his possession enraged him.

Worse, he seemed to have no way to find it again. This could have meant some sorcerer with greater powers than his own had decided to shield it from him, but that seemed most unlikely. More disturbingly, he guessed that it probably meant the crown had been returned to wherever it had been hidden for the last several millennia. Somewhere, he had to assume, inside the vast Pictish wilderness. All of his acolytes, multiplied a hundredfold, could not search that entire area.

But something had to quell his wrath. He clapped for the nearest servant, and after only a moment, a man named Debullah entered the chamber.

"My lord?" the slave said.

"Bring me a dozen slaves," al Nasir commanded. "No—twenty. Female if they're about, the younger and more beautiful the better." Debullah nodded and went to do his master's bidding without comment. Shehkmi al Nasir smiled for the first time since he'd discovered that the crown was gone. He would picture Tarawa's face while he killed the women—face-to-face, one at a time, with a sharp knife. No magic for this task. The screams of terror and pain would blunt the edge of his fury, at least for a time.

But he was not done with the Pictish prize. He vowed to remain alert for any additional news of it. And if he ever found Tarawa again, she would pay a considerable price for her complicity in its theft. But he would not obsess over the ugly thing or waste any more time now trying to find it. There were always better things he could be doing. And if he could not challenge Thoth Amon for supremacy this month, there would be many, many more opportunities in the future.

Weary or not, Shehkmi al Nasir still had centuries of life left in him. One chance had passed him by. But there would be others. He would be prepared for them.

IT WAS TIWOK, a shaman of the Raven Clan, who brought the news to Usam. "Do you feel the air?" Tiwok asked.

Usam was leaning against the log wall of a building, breathing heavily. His wounds screamed with pain, his muscles cried exhaustion, but two more of the soldiers lay dead at his feet. His war axe rested, head down, on the dirt beside him. At Tiwok's question, he paused to consider. "Warmer," he answered after a moment.

"Much warmer," the shaman said. "The Teeth of the Ice Bear is back in the cave."

"How do you know this?" Usam asked, certain the man had been nowhere near the Bear Clan village.

"That is not your concern," Tiwok said. "Only know that I do. All the shamans do."

"But . . . how is it possible?"

"You ask many questions, Usam, to which you need not know the answers."

Usam realized the shaman was right. He had not even known what function the sacred crown served until after its disappearance. If the shamans had known, they had kept quiet about it, in the manner of such people everywhere, he had no doubt. No surprise, then, that they would be equally enigmatic now.

He could not deny his own senses, however, and the warmth of the air—even a faint, sweet smell, like flowers on the wind—told him that the advance of the Ice Bear had been halted, or reversed.

"What you say seems to be true, Tiwok," he said. "But it means nothing. I have vowed to drive the Aquilonians from our lands forever."

Tiwok laughed at him. If the man hadn't been a shaman, he would have paid for that with his life, Usam thought. But the wise ones could get away with things that others could not. "That will never happen, Usam," Tiwok said. "They are innumerable. Our world is changing, and the influence of the Aquilonians—particularly under their Cimmerian king—grows every day. No empire is forever, and theirs may yet fall one day. Not in your lifetime, though, or mine. Until that day, Usam, they will be our neighbors. You might as well accustom yourself to that fact."

"Never," Usam said. The thought was repulsive to him—living in peace with those pale, civilized people? It was absurd.

"Look in your heart, and you'll see I'm right," Tiwok said. "They are too many, and more follow all the time. Our world is never stable for long, Usam. Kingdoms come and go, empires rise and fall, the sea snatches away lands even as it reveals others. We either adapt or die."

Usam wanted to argue with the holy man, but the words wouldn't come. Tiwok spoke a truth that he did not want to acknowledge. Finally, he saw the wisdom in the shaman's ideas, and he nodded glumly. "If you're right, then we have no reason to continue fighting," he said.

"Not only that, but Aquilonian troops will be here within the hour. If we stay, we'll be routed. Best to preserve as many lives as we can and go home."

Usam nodded again. Perhaps the shaman was wrong about what the future held, in which case every Pictish warrior would be needed for the next battle and the one after that. No sense letting them die for a hopeless cause when they could retreat to their own lands and wait for another chance. "Spread the word," he said. The knowledge that his brief reign as war commander of the united Pictish clans might be coming to an end made him sad, but it was tempered with happiness that the Ice Bear had been bested once again. "I will do the same. Tonight we will stay at the war camp and celebrate the crown's return. When the sun rises again we will break for our separate villages."

Tiwok agreed, and both men set out to inform the rest of their people that the war against the settlements was over. Drums would signal to those attacking Thandara.

Silently, stealthily, like ghosts—as they had come—the Pictish warriors left the settlement, melted back into the welcoming trees. Once again, Usam knew, a fragile peace would grip the land. And once again, if the Aquilonians allowed it to remain intact, so would he.

INSIDE THE GUARDIAN'S cave, Kral looked at the Teeth of the Ice Bear, resting in its proper place of honor on top of a stone pillar. He smiled with satisfaction as he regarded it. He knew that its presence there represented an accomplishment of some sort, a struggle against long odds. He could not remember the nature of that struggle, though. The sense that it had happened was a lingering memory, like the scar of a long-healed wound, of which he had many. He could not recall the circumstances behind them, either.

This did not make him unhappy. He knew that it was as it should be. The Guardian had a sacred task, and a difficult, demanding one. He would be in the cave with the crown for decades. Longer. The oldest Guardian had served for a hundred hundred years, and most stayed in the cave for well over a hundred. Kral understood that with absolute clarity—he could picture the entire history of the crown and the Guardians who had protected it before him, as readily as if it had all happened just that morning. It was the things that had occurred in his own life before he became the new Guardian that were hazy. That was so that staying in the cave would be easy for him, he realized. He would not miss aspects of his former life that he could not remember.

He sat down in a comfortable chair, carved from the very wall of the cave by the first Guardian. Each successive one had sat in this chair, and somehow it conformed to each one's anatomy as it already had to his. Still looking at the crown, still with the residual contentment of whatever he had done to restore it to the cave. While he could not recall what exactly he had done, he could feel scabs on his head, just healed, and figured they were part of the whole story. His muscles still ached from some kind of intense effort, and he derived satisfaction from that as well.

And there was something else, an image that lingered just beyond his mind's eye. He kept trying to grasp it, and failing, like trying to catch and hold a handful of river water that just kept running out between his fingers. When he could snatch a piece of it, he saw a girl with hair of the finest gold and eyes as blue as the cloudless sky. A name almost came to him, then vanished.

It didn't matter.

The fragment of an image that did come brought with it unbelievable happiness. Instead of missing her, the simple fact that he had known her was good enough. If he could just hold on to that shred of a picture, or recapture it from time to time, he could stay in the cave forever.

Kral grinned and watched the crown.

AGE OF CONAN:
HYBORIAN ADVENTURES
MARAUDERS

Volume I: GHOST OF THE WALL

Aided by a king's daughter and a circle of allies,
a young warrior embarks on a quest against those
who destroyed his people, and the tyrant who took
the precious Teeth of the Ice Bear. And to do so, he
must become his enemy's worst nightmare.
He must become a ghost.

0-441-01379-1

Volume II: WINDS OF THE WILD SEA

Young warrior Kral's search for the Teeth of the Ice
Bear—and his assaults on those who have stolen it—
have caught the attention of King Conan himself.
Now, Kral and his companions must follow the trail
of the Teeth through the back alley shadows of
Tarantia, to the halls of King Conan, and across the
seas where their greatest challenge awaits them.

0-441-01386-4

Available wherever books are sold or at
penguin.com